NEW YORK REVIEW BOOKS
CLASSICS

NADJA

ANDRÉ BRETON (1896–1966), the son of a Norman policeman and a seamstress, studied medicine in Paris and was drafted to serve in World War I in 1915. While working on a neurological ward, he met Jacques Vaché, a devotee of Alfred Jarry, and Vaché's rebellious spirit and suicide at the age of twenty-three would powerfully shape Breton's sensibility. Thanks to the auspices of Paul Valéry, Breton worked as an assistant to Marcel Proust, and in 1919, along with Philippe Soupault and Louis Aragon, he founded the journal *Littérature*. *The Magnetic Fields*, the first book of automatic writing (published by NYRB Poets), appeared in 1920, and in 1924, having broken with Tristan Tzara and the Dadaists, Breton issued the *Manifesto of Surrealism*. Among his other major works are *Anthology of Black Humor*, *Mad Love*, and *Surrealism and Painting*.

MARK POLIZZOTTI has translated more than sixty books from the French, including Arthur Rimbaud's *The Drunken Boat: Selected Writings* (NYRB Poets) and Jean Echenoz's *Command Performance* (NYRB Classics), and is the author of thirteen books, including *Revolution of the Mind: The Life of André Breton*, *Sympathy for the Traitor: A Translation Manifesto*, *Why Surrealism Matters*, and *Jump Cuts: Essays*. He lives in New York.

NADJA

ANDRÉ BRETON

Translated from the French by

MARK POLIZZOTTI

NEW YORK REVIEW BOOKS

New York

THIS IS A NEW YORK REVIEW BOOK
PUBLISHED BY THE NEW YORK REVIEW OF BOOKS
207 East 32nd Street, New York, NY 10016
www.nyrb.com

Frontispiece portrait of Nadja courtesy of Hester Albach.

Library of Congress Cataloging-in-Publication Data
Names: Breton, André, 1896–1966, author. | Polizzotti, Mark, translator, writer of introduction.
Title: Nadja / By André Breton; translated from the French by Mark Polizzotti; introduction by Mark Polizzotti.
Description: New York: New York Review Books, 2025. | Series: New York Review Books
Identifiers: LCCN 2025004091 | ISBN 9781681379364 (paperback) | ISBN 9781681379371 (ebook)
Subjects: LCGFT: Experimental fiction. | Novels.
Classification: LCC PQ2603.R35 N313 2025 | DDC 843.912—dc23/eng/20250211
LC record available at https://lccn.loc.gov/2025004091

ISBN 978-1-68137-936-4
Available as an electronic book; ISBN 978-1-68137-937-1

The authorized representative in the EU for product safety and compliance is eucomply OÜ, Pärnu mnt 139b-14, 11317 Tallinn, Estonia, hello@eucompliancepartner.com, +33 757690241.

Printed in the United States of America on acid-free paper.
10 9 8 7 6 5 4 3 2 1

CONTENTS

Nadja

INTRODUCTION
Wandering Souls

"Je ne peux finir": I can't finish. These enigmatic words, hastily scrawled on a sheet of café stationery, were the first I ever read by or about Nadja. The enticing glimpse of one of her letters to André Breton, reproduced on the cover of a French paperback, set the tone for a story that is so mysterious, so jarring, that to this day many believe it to be fiction—this, despite its author's stated disdain for "psychological literature with its novelistic fabulations."

On its surface, *Nadja* recounts Breton's chance meeting and brief relationship with a self-described "wandering soul" in the autumn of 1926. But more than this, it provides the most compelling presentation ever written of what Breton calls "the Surrealist aspiration," based on attunement to "petrifying coincidences" and the marvels of everyday life. The first third of the book, with its philosophical musings, verdicts on literary predecessors, and curated autobiographical anecdotes involving Paul Éluard, Benjamin Péret, Robert Desnos, and other future pillars of the Surrealist movement—all of which might strike readers as mere throat clearing—is in fact an essential part of Nadja's story, the context in which their meeting assumes its full significance.

Thirty years old at the time of this meeting, Breton was one of the most visible young authors on the French literary scene. His writings until then—including the automatic prose poem *The Magnetic Fields*, the essay collection *The Lost Steps*, and the *Manifesto of Surrealism*, which officially launched the movement in October 1924—were so many facets of an approach to living, one shared by Breton and his comrades in arms. The intent was not so much to create literature and art as to define, through literature and art, ways of seeing and doing that could reconnect with the lost wonder of childhood and counter centuries of rationalist thinking—the same rationalist thinking that had generated such horrors as the First World War, the repressive dominance of Catholic morality, and the wage-labor machine of capitalism. To couch this intent in purely invented terms would be beside the point, an obfuscation; rather, as Breton puts it, "I persist in demanding the names," in living "in my glass house... where I sleep at night in a glass bed under glass sheets."

To dispel all misconceptions to the contrary, then, Nadja was indeed a real woman, and this book is an *almost* entirely factual narration of a real relationship—though, as the author warns near the beginning, we should not expect "an exact account." The two met more or less as described, the nine days of their principal contact—October 4 to 12, 1926—are related in sometimes astonishing detail (the combined result of Breton's prodigious memory and timely note-taking), and, for those seeking further evidence, the volume contains forty-four documentary photographs of people, places, and items of interest, conceived from the outset as an integral element of the narrative.

Yet amid all the scrupulous documentation, one key piece is missing, one specific that would have laid to rest the decades of doubt and speculation that followed *Nadja*'s publication in 1928: the face and identity of Nadja herself. For many years, that identity was kept rigorously concealed, locked away as a shameful family secret by Nadja's heirs, as privileged information by Breton's, giving rise to various theories and assertions: that she was actually the actress Blanche Derval, who is name-checked in the book; that "Nadja" is a composite of several women, or a stand-in for Breton himself; and so on. The truth was partially revealed in 2002, when an exhibition at the Centre Pompidou displayed a hotel bill containing Nadja's family name, then more fully in 2009, after an exhaustive inquiry by the Dutch novelist Hester Albach led her to Nadja's surviving granddaughter and a cache of previously unknown records; much of the following biographical information is based on her study.

Nadja was born Léona-Camille-Ghislaine Delcourt on May 23, 1902, in the aptly named town of Saint-André, a provincial suburb of Lille, near the Belgian border. She was the third child of Eugène-Léon and Mélanie Delcourt, following an older sister, Marthe, and a brother, Charles-Camille, who had died at the age of two. Eugène had come from a comfortable bourgeois background and was, as his daughter put it, a "weak" and spoiled man. A frustrated sculptor, having squandered his fortune, he worked as a typesetter for the local newspaper—a not terribly lucrative job that didn't prevent him from indulging in luxuries the family could ill afford. Mélanie, more industrious, had fled the poverty of her Belgian village, only to find herself laboring in a textile factory from five in the morning until late at night, six days a week. Léona was recruited early on to help support the family, but from her father she also learned about the fine arts and the supposed freedoms of an artistic life. After Saint-André was liberated at the end of the First World War, the seventeen-year-old Léona fell in love with a British officer, by whom she had a daughter, named Marthe like her older sister. The officer returned to England, Léona rejected a marriage proposal by the local butcher's son, and her frantic parents offered to raise the infant on condition that the wayward teen decamp to Paris.

Lively, attractive, and curious, Léona in that spring of 1920 got her hair cut fashionably short, frequented cafés notorious for drug dealing and prostitution, and dabbled in the theater, with the vague ambition of becoming a seamstress. She had originally moved to the capital under the "protection" of an elderly industrialist (no doubt the man referred to in *Nadja* as Special Friend), who provided support in return for sexual favors, allowing Léona to bring money back to the family on her occasional visits north and to show off her chic new looks. By the time of her meeting with Breton, however, the protector and his support had evaporated, and Léona, now twenty-four, was living hand to mouth.

The attraction and fascination between Nadja and Breton seems to have been immediate and mutual. "I had never seen such eyes," Breton writes of their initial encounter. "What can be going on in those eyes that is so extraordinary?" For her part, Nadja later wrote to Breton: "I recall the powerful image of our meeting... I see you walking toward me with that ray of gentle grandeur clinging to the locks of your hair ——and your godlike gaze." Irresistibly drawn but "expecting the worst" (that is, fearing she might be a prostitute), Breton invited the woman to a café. As if nothing were more natural for her than these chance encounters, she told him of her parents, her home in northern France, a boy she'd loved and left behind. She called herself Nadja, she said, "because in Russian it's the beginning of the word for hope, and because it's only the beginning." (In fact, the name was most likely taken from the American music hall artist Beatrice

Wagner, who at the time performed under the stage name Nadja the Topless Dancer.) Over the next nine days, the two met daily, sometimes by arrangement, sometimes by accident, their words and interactions marked by a potent mix of wonder, synchronicity, and, at times, tedium—for Breton's account does not avoid the moments when he found Nadja's monologues tiresome, her behavior incomprehensible or simply irritating. The relationship soon turned physical, progressing from kisses in a taxi to a night in an out-of-town hotel.

What were they seeking in each other? Breton's first-person account states unambiguously that, for him, Nadja's way of being—her unearthly nonchalance regarding people, her name, even herself; her unpredictable wanderings; her seeming obliviousness to money and accepted custom; and most of all her utterances, a disquieting combination of the frivolous and the oracular—responded to an ideal that he had only partially glimpsed before this. Entranced by the woman's acute intuition, her sometimes frightening ability to connect with his own thoughts, and what he took to be her unfettered lifestyle (which only partially masked a desperation to stay afloat in a city that had left her adrift), he describes her as "a free genius, like one of those ethereal spirits that certain magic practices allow you to engage with momentarily but that you could never subdue." As for Nadja, it's possible that Breton was at first for her a potential means of support, another "protector," and she does not hide her dismay when he mentions being married. But whatever her initial feelings or ambitions, she soon became engulfed in the attentions Breton paid her, trying with increasing anxiety to hold his interest even as he began pulling away. Though their first sexual encounter was followed by others, as Nadja's letters make clear, the emotional investment was lopsided: the sad fact seems to be that by year's end, while Nadja was suffering the torments of unfulfilled passion, Breton, whose marriage was faltering, seems mainly to have been stroking his ego. In November, he sadly reported to his wife, Simone Kahn Breton, who had been privy to their story since the beginning, that Nadja had fallen in love with him "in that grave and desperate way that perhaps I impose on her," even as he guiltily acknowledged that "I do not love the woman, and in all likelihood I never will. She is only capable... of putting in doubt everything I do love and my way of loving. No less dangerous for all that." More dismissively, he remarked to a friend that sex with Nadja "was like making love to Joan of Arc."

"Can it be that this frantic pursuit ends here?" Breton asks after the culmination of their nine-day journey. Yes and no. Though their daily meetings had come to an end, the two remained in contact until the following March. Perhaps hoping to rediscover what had initially captivated him, Breton suggested publishing a book of Nadja's writings and drawings, and asked to borrow her journals. But the fascination of the early days was gone, and more often than not their time together devolved into bitter spats.

Moreover, Breton found Nadja's journals a disappointment, and the publication project fell by the wayside. Angry and offended, Nadja demanded them back: "Why did you force me to hand over my little kitchen sink woes—André, I knew it——you found it all rather pedestrian." And while Breton had earlier communicated his excitement to his friends—the Surrealist writer Pierre Naville recalled that Nadja "was at first the subject of a collective emotion, the kind Breton was so good at inspiring"—she now became a source of embarrassment. On one occasion, Breton brought Nadja unannounced to the Galerie Surréaliste, the group's exhibition and gathering space, on a day when Naville and Simone were present: "She truly is a strange woman," Naville reported. "Fantastic eyes that change shape, and talking exactly as [Breton] said." At the same time, he couldn't help noticing that Breton had begun to "lose patience with her." Nadja herself appeared ill at ease in front of Simone, "not knowing what tone (what words) to use when talking about André."

As autumn turned to winter, Nadja's financial situation grew increasingly dire. Wishing to please Breton, she had stopped resorting to her former means of obtaining money (gifts from admirers, at least one instance of drug trafficking). She spent the Christmas season of 1926, at his urging, going from one squalid hotel to another in search of cheaper accommodations, finally settling on the Hôtel Becquerel in Montmartre, not far from the Bretons' apartment on rue Fontaine. Several times in the book, Breton speaks of helping Nadja as much as his own finances would allow, once selling a Derain from his and Simone's collection to pay her rent. "The vacant space this painting leaves on the wall will be a thousand times more precious than the painting itself," he rationalized to his wife.

Nadja's letters to Breton during those months, by turns fraught, seductive, furious, and pragmatic, and fluctuating between an intimate *tu* and a formal *vous*, form a litany of emotional highs and lows, as she vacillated between desolation at having lost her lover's attentions, rage at feeling abandoned, outright fantasy, and rekindled hope in their shared future. Late October 1926: "It's cold when I'm alone. I'm afraid of myself——When you're here——the sky belongs to the two of us . . . André—I love you—Why, oh why have you stolen my eyes." November 15: "I am just a tiny thing, inert and lost . . . I remain here suspended in this dream . . . waiting for a confession——the tenderest confession of my life . . . you are there—but death is there too—yes it is there behind you—but no matter / *I can't finish*." Late November: "I walk down your street 6 times a day—without the joy of getting a glimpse of you." November 30: "Understand this letter with the end of my breath—for it's the beginning of yours." December 1: "I'm enjoying myself like a little girl surrounded by her playthings . . . I also sing——what difference does it make. I'll see you soon, won't I?—and then I'll be good—like a well-behaved toy." December 2: "The path of our kisses was so beautiful, wasn't it——and Satan so tempting." December 11: "Wildcat with saber teeth . . . His Nadja begs him. But seized by a mad desire—too long repressed, he suddenly draws her to him—and tenderly crushes her to his bare chest . . ." December 23: "I've lost—it was in the cards, wasn't it——you said so! And that's not all. Fate is conspiring against me. I was turned out of my hotel this morning . . . and since you are righteous and well ordered—you will now lump me in with the other lowlifes." December 31: "My Flame—I wanted to telephone you but, I'm too nervous and afraid of feeling your anxiety . . . you know I am your slave and you are my everything but I want more I want to take on all your troubles—suffer in your stead. I want you to be happy." January 3, 1927: "What can I tell you that you don't already know in spite of everything——you——and me——you're leaving me far too alone my friend——and I am congested with stifled desires . . . Ah monster——what are you doing to my life? . . . [My hotel] is not far from you! Not even 5 minutes by taxi. So I really can't understand why you haven't *come*." January 15: "It's now been 12 days since the last time we met——I don't know if you want this to last forever——...How good it is to remember——here you were——I'm there now. My mouth glued lovingly to the pillow, where your stern ears were resting—and I'm talking I'm telling you the things my emotions kept me from saying when you were here—And I look around suddenly, amazed at finding myself alone." January 20: "What a lovely day, André, I've just awoken entirely transformed, and it feels so light to breathe in this beautiful sky, that I feel as if I've been transported elsewhere...Why did it all have to darken into bitter necessities—Forgive me, André——I was worthy of you when I pushed you away...I want to win your respect—I'll change my life if necessary." January 28: "We can never forget that——understanding—that union——and yet that floating support transformed me so completely that I don't recognize myself...I feel lost if you abandon me...I'm like a dove wounded by the lead she carries in herself." January 29: "You haven't called me—You surely have better things to do. Perhaps just as well. And yet André—I have something to ask you. Can you help me out one more time—I'm not hoping for anything, from anyone—except from you—whatever little you can send me will be timely. Perhaps the day will come when I can repay everything you've done for me. Please believe that I'm only writing out of urgent need...Place me with one of your friends—No matter who—I'll do whatever is necessary—anything at all...It's raining still / My room is dark / Heart in the abyss / My sanity is dying." January 31, having received his damning appraisal of her notebook entries: "I got your bludgeon of a note...You made me into something so beautiful—André—I feel lighthearted in spite of everything. But I'm angry at you. Why did you destroy the other 2 Nadjas?" February 2 or 3: "I want to have a serious talk with you. You like to play at being cruel—it suits you well—I assure you—but I am not a toy——and besides it's not polite... I want my notebook back——however 'plain vanilla' it might seem to you... Too bad—in the end you are just like all the rest——and you do no honor to what you've created——Personally, I'd rather preserve my illusions in spite of everything... I see things very differently from you and your retinue—I despise your games—your clique... I wasn't very useful to you, was I—But I gave you the deepest and best of myself——to the point of forgetting about my own daughter——How horrible—and I resent you for it." February 4: "My André—I love you, you know that... you live in me—but don't monopolize me too much. You know very well that your claws leave traces. Like your thoughts, which plunge me into darkness... I dreamed about a necklace of pearls shaped like your teeth." February 18: "I'm astounded that you haven't replied to my last letter——Nevertheless I want my notebook back—and I can't understand why you're keeping it from me... You can bring it to me here——if you deem me worthy of the slight inconvenience—just as a friend—if you wish you can wear a blindfold!!!" Finally, in late February or early March, a downcast but defiantly optimistic farewell, slipped under the door of the Bretons' apartment:

> Thank you, André, I've received everything. I have confidence in the image that will shut my eyes. I feel connected to you by something very powerful; perhaps this trial was the necessary beginning of a higher event. I have faith in you... I don't want to waste any of the time you'll need for loftier things—Whatever you do

> will be done well—Let nothing stop you—There are enough people whose mission it is to *put out the Flame*... Every day thought is renewed——It's wise not to dwell on the impossible—But one must get beyond it. André, despite everything I am part of you—It's more than love. It's Strength, and I believe.

This was Nadja's last communication with Breton, but not her last writing to him. On March 14, an unsent draft shows evidence of a precarious emotional state:

> Go today tomorrow morning. You'll come to [café] terminus. I'll be there. We have to make sure to place ourselves side by side—and alone. The godlike look belongs to you. Trifle. Toward you all forces will converge. I don't believe in those. People believe in yours, too bad for you. It's proven, I'm sure of it. Have you had a good education (average). Do you know your geography (no). Are you a good psychologist? (fairly good). Can you inform us immediately (no). What do you want as a guarantee? I don't know what you want from me.

One week later, Nadja was discovered screaming in terror in the corridor of her hotel, having seen men on the roof (in an ironic echo of a scene Breton reports in the book—and which might in fact have been workmen on the neighboring rooftop, rather than the hallucination commonly supposed). She was brought to the police prefecture in Place Dauphine (another ironic echo) and committed to Sainte-Anne mental hospital that same day, with a lengthy diagnosis that included anxiety, manic depression, and the conviction that outside forces were sending her odors and shooting electricity through her body; three days later, she was admitted to the Perray-Vaucluse hospital in the southern Paris suburb of Épinay-sur-Orge. Breton, learning of Nadja's internment—and despite a long-standing assumption to the contrary, as well as his own representation in the book—apparently tried to visit her, as evidenced by an undated letter to him from a Dr. Gilbert Robin, but without success. Nadja's parents, on the other hand, did travel to Perray-Vaucluse, on March 27, and spent the next fourteen months petitioning her doctors to send their daughter closer to home. Finally, on May 16, 1928, one week shy of her twenty-sixth birthday, Léona Delcourt was transferred to the psychiatric hospital in Bailleul, about twenty miles from Saint-André, with a diagnosis of schizophrenia. Nine days later, *Nadja* was published by the prestigious literary house of Gallimard.

Although the Bailleul hospital prided itself on being a model institution, its touted amenities were mainly reserved for wealthier clients. For those less fortunate, being treated at the Bailleul was like traveling in steerage: the undertrained, underpaid medical staff meted out abusive treatments or ignored the patients altogether. Léona, pegged as a difficult case—her chart mentions episodes of bed-wetting, screaming and cursing, exhibitionism, hallucinations, and physical violence (little wonder, given the conditions in which she lived)—was subjected to frequent punishment. On one visit, her parents and daughter, Marthe, now fourteen, found her and ten other patients locked into tubs of freezing, filthy water, howling to be let out; in horror, Marthe fled the hospital and never saw her mother again. When the Second World War broke out, much of the staff also fled, leaving the inmates prey to severe shortages as the occupying German forces commandeered what few resources remained.

Over the course of those months, Léona's sporadic records indicate a rapid decline in her physical and mental well-being, the result of sustained mistreatment, malnourishment, and privation. She died in the Bailleul on January 15, 1941, at the age of thirty-eight, having succumbed to a possible cancerous tumor and to indisputable neglect.

Breton had begun taking notes on his encounters with Nadja soon after the halt in their relations in October, but it wasn't until August of the following year that he began to work in earnest on a book about her. The idea had occurred early, to both of them. "André? André? . . . You'll write a novel about me," Breton reports Nadja saying. "Beware: everything fades, everything disappears. Something of us must remain . . . You'll find a Latin or Arabic pseudonym. Promise me. You have to." And, in a letter: "You'll use me and I'll do my best to help you make something good." But Breton wanted none of pseudonyms or novels, and when Nadja saw his notes for the book, her reaction was one of shock and hurt. "How could you write such mean-spirited deductions of *what we were* without the breath leaving your body?" she wrote him on November 1. "And how could I read this report——glimpse this distorted portrait of myself, without rebelling, or even weeping?"

Breton's life at this time was one of conflict and distraction. His attempts since 1925 to make common cause with the French Communist Party, including briefly joining the Party itself, frequently ran afoul of the Communists' skepticism toward the Surrealists, whom they considered mere bourgeois dilettantes. These tumultuous dealings had reached a crisis point in late 1926 and early 1927, which partly (but not entirely) explains the infrequency of Breton's visits to Nadja, as lamented in her letters. At the same time, Breton's marriage to Simone was foundering, due in part to his long and unrequited infatuation with the poet and socialite Lise Meyer (later Lise Deharme), the "lady of the glove" mentioned in *Nadja*—an infatuation that lasted nearly three years, during which time Breton lurched from hope to despair, each mood swing duly reported to his tolerant wife.

It was both to be near Lise, who was renting a house in nearby Pourville, and to begin writing *Nadja* that Breton, in early August 1927, took a room alone in the Norman resort town of Varengeville-sur-Mer at the Manoir d'Ango, a sixteenth-century château, famous for its magnificent tiled dovecote and loggia, that now served as a tourist inn. Work got off to a slow start: his first two weeks at the manor were mainly spent reading—novels by Huysmans, a memoir of Victor Hugo—and visiting or receiving visits from friends, including his closest confidant, Louis Aragon, who was vacationing nearby and working on his own book, the sulfuric diatribe *Treatise on Style*. The fact that Aragon could toss off ten or fifteen pages in a day to his friend's one or two further lowered Breton's spirits.

Nonetheless, by mid-month he had begun drafting the opening episodes, reporting to Simone that the "generalities around Nadja" were "fairly interesting. I speak pretty coherently of things that are, I believe, rather exceptional." Taking his cue from Freud's case studies, Breton intended to create an atmosphere of clinical objectivity, later explaining that "the tone adopted for this narrative is copied from the one used in medical observations . . . without seeking to give its expression the least stylistic polish." Still, however objective the surface, the drama of his relations with Nadja remains undimmed.

By September, Breton was back in Paris, having finished all but the concluding section. Encouraged by his friends' enthusiastic reactions to the manuscript, he began gathering images to complement the text: Man Ray, the group's unofficial portraitist, was commissioned to photograph individual Surrealists, while Ray's assistant, Jacques-André Boiffard, matched Breton's unadorned prose with eerily depopulated cityscapes (uncredited). Breton also began planning the third and final part, intended as a meditation on beauty—until a sudden disruption in his life yanked the book in an unexpected direction.

In November, Breton met with the writer Emmanuel Berl to discuss a joint publishing venture. Berl arrived at the meeting accompanied by his mistress, a "tall, slender, gracefully shaped" young woman (as one Surrealist described her) "with regular, slightly Nordic features . . . Very flirtatious and attractive." It took only that one café meeting and a dinner at Éluard's for Breton to fall desperately in love.

Suzanne Fernande Muzard was born on September 26, 1900. Determined to leave behind the poverty of her youth, she had arrived in Paris three years earlier and gravitated to the brothel La Ruchette, where Berl had found her on one of his visits. He had settled her in his comfortable apartment and, as part of her "education," given her books to read, among them the unfinished manuscript of *Nadja*, which he wanted to publish. Seduced by the book, Suzanne had asked Berl to introduce her to its author.

Within days, Breton had convinced Muzard to run away with him to the South, a trip he related to Simone in a series of long letters. "Suzanne is utterly exquisite," he raved from a Toulon hotel. "This is the first time in a week I've left her side for even ten minutes." But the idyll was short-lived: Suzanne had not let passion blind her to practical realities, and at the end of their trip she demanded that Breton leave his wife and marry her instead: "All or nothing." Breton, unprepared for the thought of divorcing Simone, went home to rue Fontaine while Suzanne took a hotel room. Seizing his chance, Berl offered to take Suzanne abroad—but not before Breton, hearing of the departure at the last minute, rushed with several friends to the Gare de Lyon in an effort to stop them. Suzanne hesitated, impressed by this show of force on her behalf; but, urged on by Berl, she finally let the train carry her away.

It was after this incident that Breton wrote the conclusion to *Nadja*, centered on his meeting with and loss of his new beloved. Addressed only as "you," Muzard comes to embody for Breton the summation and justification of Nadja's clouded signal, the marvelous creature that Nadja had unwittingly prophesied. And just as he magnified Nadja, so now he magnified Suzanne, turning the book's final pages into a manifesto on the power of beauty and sudden chance occurrences, ending with the now-famous credo: "Beauty will be CONVULSIVE or not at all." More privately, Breton used his pages to rewrite events of the preceding days, casting beauty as "a train ceaselessly lurching from the Gare de Lyon, but that I know will never leave, has never left." In this alternate reality, subject to the logic of desire rather than of practicalities, Suzanne had not departed with his rival but rather stayed behind to consummate a passion without end. Reflecting on these pages several years later, Breton wrote that his relationship with Muzard "did not entirely kill in me the man to whom a vanishing Nadja, by a miracle of grace and selflessness, had perhaps entrusted her. That man... can imagine no disappointment in love, but he imagines and has never stopped imagining life—in its continuity—as the locus of every disappointment. It's already rather curious, rather interesting that it should be so..."

From nearly the moment of its publication, *Nadja* became Breton's most popular book, and today enjoys a reputation as the most famous literary work to come out of Surrealism. All well and good, but time, and the intensive research that fascination with Breton's account and its heroine has inspired, have also laid bare some problematic aspects. For all its purported factuality, Breton's narrative contains a number of inconsistencies.* And despite his absorbing presentation of an exceptional woman, his story of Nadja is really the story of himself, of his frantic, relentless, sometimes oblivious pursuit of a world governed by marvels and not misery, in which Léona Delcourt becomes something of a philosophical stand-in, more embodiment than body. Because of his selective descriptions, the theorizing and conceptual airbrushing surrounding them, Breton has often been accused—I did so in my biography of him—of turning Nadja into a symbol, denaturing her, as Nadja herself charged in her letter of November 1. And there is no doubt that the

*To take one example, the manuscript of *Nadja* places their meeting on October 3, a Sunday, which Breton crossed out and replaced with Monday the 4th. Had he misremembered, or did it better suit his purpose to link his meeting with Nadja to his thoughts about office workers, which would be more apropos on a weekday? Similarly, in her letter of January 20, Nadja recalls meeting Breton "near the Saint-Georges metro," next to Trinité church, whereas Breton's description places them near the church of Saint-Vincent-de-Paul and the Poissonnière metro, several stops farther east.

power dynamics between André—an established public intellectual, relatively comfortable if not exactly well off—and Léona—impoverished, infatuated, desperate—were anything but balanced. Still, I can't help agreeing with Hester Albach's argument that to label Nadja a victim "both does an injustice to Léona and underestimates Breton." While *Nadja* offers a weighted version of the facts, in which the physical reality of Léona Delcourt risks becoming subsumed under the more wraithlike, almost spectral appearance of her chosen persona, it is also the case that the book brings to life a fully realized, engaging, desiring, extraordinarily touching and charismatic woman.

This is one of the reasons why *Nadja* continues to fascinate one hundred years after its first publication. A second is the resonant and enchanting portrait it offers of Paris, the book's other major protagonist: an alternate Paris hidden in the day-to-day city, bristling with uncharted wonders, unexpected encounters, and disturbing, enticing spaces. On both these levels, the book remains an extraordinary writerly feat: once inside Breton and Nadja's peculiar reality, with its mesmerizing events and petrifying coincidences, its dialogues that you can practically *hear* from the page, it becomes extremely difficult to leave. If *Nadja* is still worth reading, it is both for the bewitching qualities of its larger-than-life heroine and for the indelible portrait that Breton created of her, of himself, and of a city in which it was still possible to envision marvelous occurrences.

This translation is based on the original 1928 edition of *Nadja*. Breton returned to the book more than three decades later, making a number of minor and not so minor alterations to the text and illustrations for a revised edition that was published in 1963. Among other things, he obscured the nature of his relations with Nadja, including their sexual encounter, and erased from the narrative several figures who had since fallen out of favor (or, conversely, removed some disobliging remarks, such as his snipe at Tristan Tzara, in the wake of their subsequent reconciliation). The main revisions are indicated in the endnotes to this volume.

The previous English translation of *Nadja*, by Richard Howard, was first published in English in 1960 and has been in print ever since. So why another one? Howard was a poet above all, and his translation contains many beautiful wordings, some of which I've retained when I didn't feel they could be bettered. Still, despite my great respect for his work, I find that his version of *Nadja* contains a surprising number of mistranslations and misreadings. On top of which, his language often strikes me as more convoluted than necessary. Breton was a complex stylist—the term he used for his sentences and thinking was "serpentine"—but he also had a message to convey. While endeavoring to preserve the sinuosity of Breton's phrasings, I've also labored to make them, and his overall intention in *Nadja*, more comprehensible in English than has been the case.

In addition, we now know much more about both the book and its subject than was available to scholars sixty-five years ago, and I have benefited from recent materials, as well as from the research I undertook when writing Breton's biography, *Revolution of the Mind*, to help inform me about some of the more obscure passages in this narrative. The endnotes are aimed at helping contemporary English-language readers navigate the references and detours in the text, many of which their French counterparts of a century ago would have grasped more readily.

I'm indebted to Jacqueline Colliss Harvey, Edwin Frank, Deborah Karl, Alex Andriesse, Hasan Altaf, and James Brook for their careful reading of this translation, as well as to the following works, which provided much essential information: André Breton, *Œuvres complètes*, vol. 1, ed. Marguerite Bonnet (Paris, 1988); Hester Albach, *Léona, héroïne du surréalisme* (Arles, 2009); André Breton, *Lettres à Simone Kahn, 1920–1960*, ed. Jean-Michel Goutier (Paris, 2016); Jacqueline Chénieux-Gendron and Olivier Wagner, *Nadja en silence*, and the accompanying facsimile of the *Nadja* manuscript (Paris, 2019); Isabelle Diu et al., *L'Invention du surréalisme: Des Champs magnétiques à Nadja* (Paris, 2020); and Sylvain Amic and Alexandre Mare, eds., *Nadja, un itinéraire surréaliste* (Paris and Rouen, 2022). Nadja's letters to Breton can be accessed at https://www.andrebreton.fr/en/series/222.

—MARK POLIZZOTTI

NADJA

ILLUSTRATIONS

WHO AM I? If for once I were to fall back on a proverb—then why shouldn't everything come down to knowing whom I "haunt"? I admit that this last word baffles me, as it seems to establish between certain individuals and myself relations that are more singular, inevitable, and disturbing than I'd realized. It says much more than it intends, makes me play the part of a ghost while still alive; it naturally alludes to what I had to stop being, in order to become *who* I am. Taken in an only slightly aberrant sense, it makes me understand that what I consider the objective, and more or less deliberate, manifestations of my existence in fact derive—within the confines of this life—from an activity whose true scope is utterly unknown to me. My conception of "ghosts," its conventionality in both appearance and blind submission to certain contingencies of time and place, is, to my mind, mainly worthwhile as the finite image of a potentially eternal torment. It's possible that my life is but an image of this type, and that I am doomed to retrace my steps, all the while believing I'm moving forward; doomed to try to know what I should already recognize, to relearn a tiny portion of what I've forgotten. This view of myself seems false only insofar as it *presupposes* me, arbitrarily placing in the past a former way of thinking that shouldn't be subject to time and implying—in this same time—a sense of irreparable loss, of penitence or fall, whose lack of moral validity I consider beyond question. What matters most is that the specific aptitudes I've gradually discovered in myself should not distract me from seeking a more general aptitude, one that would be mine alone and is not inherent. Beyond any preferences I recognize I have, affinities I feel, attractions I suffer, events that happen to me and only to me; beyond any number of actions I see myself committing, emotions I'm alone in experiencing—beyond these, I endeavor to know what my difference vis-à-vis others consists of, if not what it stems from. Isn't it precisely to the degree that I realize this difference that I will discover what I, and I alone, have come into this world to accomplish, what unique message I'm bearing, for whose fate I am solely responsible?

On the basis of such reflections, I would like it if critics limited themselves—and while this does mean relinquishing their most cherished prerogatives, it would ultimately offer them a less futile goal than mechanically clarifying others' ideas—to making informed incursions into the domain they believe wholly forbidden to them, the domain external to the work, in which the individual author, coping with the minutiae of daily existence, expresses himself in complete abandon and often so distinctively. I recall this anecdote: Victor Hugo, toward the end of his life, riding for the thousandth time with Juliette Drouet and interrupting his silent meditation only when their carriage passed by a property with two gates, one large and one small, to point out the larger one to Juliette: "Carriage gate, madam," at which she pointed to the smaller one and replied: "Pedestrian gate, sir"; then, a bit farther on, before two trees with intertwined branches: "Philemon and Baucis," knowing that this time Juliette would not respond—that, and the assurance we're given that this marvelous, poignant ceremony was repeated day after day for years on end: How could any study of Hugo, no matter how subtle, tell us as much, make us feel as much, about what he was, and is? Those two gates are like the mirror of his strength and his weakness, though it's unclear which one represents his pettiness and which his greatness. And what difference could all the genius in the world make if he did not admit that adorable correction, expressive of love and entirely contained in Juliette's rejoinder? Hugo's most astute and enthusiastic commentator will never share anything with me that could match that supreme sense of *proportion*.

I'd be thrilled to have a private document of this caliber for every figure I admire. Failing that, I can still make do with documents of lesser value, however insufficient in emotional terms. I do not admire Flaubert, and yet, if told that by his own admission he wanted, in *Salammbô*, merely to "give the impression of the color yellow" and, in *Madame Bovary*, to "create something that is the color of mold in corners that harbor wood lice," and that he didn't care about the rest, these essentially extraliterary preoccupations would not leave me indifferent. For me, the magnificent light in Courbet's paintings is the same as in Place Vendôme, at the hour when the column fell. In the present day, if a man like de Chirico were to reveal what had once motivated him—fully and of course without artifice, in the most stringent and unnerving detail—what a giant leap forward for exegesis that would be! Without him (or rather, in spite of him), and based solely on his earlier canvases and a handwritten notebook I have in my possession, we might reconstruct the universe that was his until 1917, but only partially. It is one of my great regrets not to be able to fill in the gaps, not to fully grasp everything that, in such a universe, goes against the natural order, establishes a new scale of things. De Chirico recognized back then that he could paint only when *surprised* (he first of all) by certain arrangements of objects, and that the whole enigma of revelation was contained for him in the word *surprise*. To be sure, the work that resulted from it remained "closely linked to the circumstance that provoked its birth" but resembled it only "in a strange way, like the resemblance between two brothers, or rather between the image of someone we know seen in a dream, and that person in reality; it is, and at the same time it is not, the same person; it is as if there had been a slight and mysterious transfiguration of the features." Along with dispositions of objects that struck de Chirico as especially blatant, we would also have to train our critical attention on the objects themselves, to study why such a small number of them were always being used in these groupings. We will know nothing about de Chirico until we've elucidated his innermost views on the artichoke, the glove, the biscuit, or the spindle. If only we could have his cooperation on this score! As far as I'm concerned, the mind's disposition toward certain objects is even more important than its attitude toward certain dispositions of objects, those two types of dispositions alone governing every form of sensibility.

In this vein, I find I have so much in common with Huysmans, the Huysmans of *En rade* and *Là-bas*—in his way of evaluating whatever presents itself, of selecting with the partiality of despair from among what *is*—that while sadly I know him only through his writings, he is perhaps less of a stranger to me than any of my friends. But also, hasn't he, more than anyone, taken to extremes the necessary, *vital* distinction between the ring, so fragile in appearance, that could be our life preserver and the dizzying conspiracy of forces that threaten to drag us down? He revealed to me the resounding boredom that virtually every spectacle inspired in him. While he could not quite show me the dawning of the unpremeditated over the ravaged fields of conscious possibility, he was at least the first to convince me of its absolute human inevitability and of the uselessness of seeking loopholes for myself. I am hugely indebted to him for telling me, regardless of its effect, about everything that concerned and preoccupied him, his darkest moments of distress, from outside that distress; for not "singing" absurdly of that distress like so many poets but rather enumerating, patiently and in the shadows, the few small, wholly involuntary reasons he could find for existing, and for being—for whose benefit, he couldn't say—the person speaking! He, too, is the object of one of those persistent calls that seem to come from beyond and that momentarily freeze us before chance arrangements of a fairly novel type, whose secret we could discover were we to look deep within ourselves. In the same way, I set him apart (need it be said) from those empirical fiction writers who claim to stage characters that are unlike them, portraying them—physically and psychologically, as they do—for the needs of some pointless cause! Out of one real person, about whom they believe they know something, they make two characters in their story; out of two, they make one. And people bother to discuss it! Someone suggested to an author I know, about a book of his that was about to be published in which the heroine might too easily be recognized, that he should at least *also* change the color of her hair. As a blond, apparently, she would not have given away the brunette. Well, I don't find that infantile, I find it monstrous. I persist in demanding the names, in being interested only in books left swinging like doors, for which you don't need to find the key. Thank goodness the days are numbered for psychological literature with its novelistic fabulations. No question that it was Huysmans who dealt it the fatal blow.

As for me, I'll continue to live in my glass house, where at all hours you can see who comes to visit, where everything hanging from the ceiling and on the walls is held there as if by magic, where I sleep at night in a glass bed under glass sheets, where *who I am* will sooner or later appear to me etched by a diamond. To be sure, and here again, nothing captivates me as much as the complete disappearance of Lautréamont behind his work, and I constantly have in mind his terrifying "tics, tics, and tics." But there remains, for me, something supernatural in the circumstances of so complete a human erasure. It would be all too vain to try to match it, and I'm readily convinced that this ambition, on the part of those who retreat behind it, expresses nothing very honorable. Mr. Tristan Tzara would no doubt prefer it not be known that at the performance of his *Bearded Heart*, in Paris, he "gave" Paul Éluard and me up to the police, when a spontaneous gesture of that sort is so deeply significant, and that in this light, which cannot fail to be the light of posterity, *25 Poems* (the title of one of his books) becomes *25 Police Rantings*.

I intend to relate, in the margins of the narrative that I have yet to begin, only the most striking episodes of my life *such as I can conceive of it apart from its organic plan*, and indeed insofar as it is subject to chance, both great and small; of my life as it briefly eludes my control, introduces me into an almost forbidden world which is that of sudden parallels, of petrifying coincidences, of reflexes that belong to every individual, of harmonies banged down as if on a piano, of flashes that would let you see, really *see*, if they didn't flit by even more rapidly than the others. These are facts whose intrinsic value is totally unverifiable; facts which, because of their absolutely unexpected, violently incidental nature, and the suspect associations of ideas they provoke—a way of making you pass from the gossamer thread to the spider's web, in other words to what would be the most scintillating and graceful thing in the world, if in the corner, or the vicinity, a spider wasn't lurking—might be on the order of pure observation but which in every case appear as a signal, without our being able to say exactly what kind of signal; facts which allow me to enjoy unlikely complicities even in total solitude, which convince me of my error when I occasionally fear I'm standing alone at the helm. It would be worth establishing a hierarchy of such facts, from the simplest to the most complex: starting with the special, undefinable reaction provoked by the sight of very rare objects or our arrival in a particular place, accompanied by the clear sensation that something momentous and essential depends on it, and ending with the complete absence of tranquility that certain enchantments, certain coincidences that surpass our understanding, cause in us, and that most often allow us to resume rational activity only if we heed our instinct for self-preservation. We could place quite a few intermediaries between these *slippage-facts* and these *precipice-facts*. Between the one type of facts, to which I can only bear frantic witness, and the other type, of which I have the weakness to believe that I've fully grasped the ins and outs, there might be the same distance as between a statement or group of statements that constitute a so-called surrealist sentence or text, and the statement or group of statements that, for the same observer, constitute a sentence or text whose every term he has carefully weighed and considered. In the first instance, he does not seem to feel responsible, so to speak; in the second, he does. He is, on the other hand, infinitely more amazed and fascinated by what's happening in the former than in the latter. He is also prouder of it, which is rather strange; he feels freer because of it. At issue are those elective sensations I spoke of, whose very share of incommunicability is a source of unequaled pleasure.

Do not expect from me an exact account of what I've had the opportunity to experience in this domain. I will limit myself here to recalling without undue effort what has sometimes happened to me, through none of my own doing; what, arriving via unsuspected routes, has given me the measure of the particular grace and disgrace that concern me. I will speak of these instances in no predetermined order, following the momentary whim that lets things bubble up as they will. I'll take as my point of departure the Hôtel des Grands Hommes on Place du Panthéon, where I lived around 1918, and as a stopover, the Manoir d'Ango in Varengeville-sur-Mer, where I find myself in August 1927, decidedly unchanged—the Manoir d'Ango, where they offered to put me up, when I didn't wish to be disturbed, in a hut at the edge of a wood, hidden by a factitious row of shrubs, and where, while doing as I pleased, I could also indulge in hunting with eagle owls. (Could it possibly have been otherwise, since I planned to write *Nadja*?) In truth, it hardly matters if an error, omission, utter confusion, or actual oversight should occasionally cast a shadow on what I'm relating—on what, overall, should be considered unimpeachable. Finally, I'd rather that such accidents of thought not be reduced to their *unjust* proportion of random anecdotes, and if I say,

I'll take as my point of departure the Hôtel des Grands Hommes . . . (p. 10)

The Manoir d'Ango in Varengeville-sur-Mer (p. 10)

If I say, for instance, that in Paris the statue of Étienne Dolet in Place Maubert has always both attracted me and caused me an unbearable malaise... (p. 10)

for instance, that in Paris the statue of Étienne Dolet in Place Maubert has always both attracted me and caused me an unbearable malaise, you not immediately deduce that I'm ripe for psychoanalysis—a method that I respect, that I think aims at nothing less than ejecting man from himself, and from which I anticipate more than just bailiff's writs. Besides, I'm fairly sure that psychoanalysis is not yet qualified to deal with such phenomena, since, despite its many merits, we'd be giving it too much credit in saying that it has fully explored the question of dreams, or that its interpretations of "slips" do not simply occasion further slips.

Which brings me to my own experience—to what is, for me, about myself, a virtually continuous subject of meditation and reverie:

The day Apollinaire's play *Color of Time* was first performed, at the Renée Maubel Conservatory, as I was chatting with Picasso in the balcony during intermission, a young man came up to me and stammered out a few words, finally managing to explain that he had mistaken me for a friend whom he'd believed lost in the war. Naturally, it went no further. Not long afterward, via a mutual acquaintance, I began corresponding with Paul Éluard, whom I didn't know by sight. He came to see me while on leave: I found myself in the presence of the same person as at *Color of Time*.

The words WOOD & COAL spread across the last page of *The Magnetic Fields* caused me, one entire Sunday when I was out walking with Soupault, to exercise a bizarre talent for predicting every shop designated by those words. No

Paul Éluard (Photo by Man Ray) (p. 14)

The words WOOD & COAL (p. 14)

matter which street we started down, I seemed to be able to say exactly where, on the right or left, such a shop would appear. And I was proved right every time. I was informed, guided, not by a hallucinatory vision of the words in question but rather by the image of one of those coarsely painted slices of wood, of uniform color except for a dark center, shown in section in small stacks on the facade, on either side of the door. Once back home, that image continued to haunt me. A merry-go-round melody, coming from carrefour Médicis, again affected me as if it were that log. As did the scalp of Jean-Jacques Rousseau, whose statue I could see from my window, from the back, two or three stories below. That day, I was very frightened.

Again in my room on Place du Panthéon, one evening, late. Someone knocks. A woman enters, whose approximate age and features I've now forgotten. Dressed in mourning, I think. She asks for an issue of the magazine *Littérature* that isn't out yet and that someone made her promise to bring back to Nantes the next day. Despite my reluctance, she insists on having it. Mostly, she seems to have come to "recommend" the person sending her, who will soon be moving to Paris. (I still recall the expression: "Who would like to embark on a literary career," which since then, knowing whom it concerned, I've found so curious, so touching.) But who was I being asked, in this quixotic way, to welcome and advise? Several days later, Benjamin Péret was there.

Nantes: perhaps the only city in France, along with Paris, where I get the sense that something worthwhile might

Several days later, Benjamin Péret was there (Photo by Man Ray) (p. 17)

happen to me; where certain gazes burn too brightly, strictly for themselves (I noticed this again last year while driving through Nantes, when I spotted a woman, a laborer, I believe, who was with a man, and who raised her eyes: I should have stopped); where for me the cadence of life is not like anywhere else; where a spirit of adventure beyond any other still inhabits certain individuals. Nantes, from where friends might still come; Nantes, where I loved a park: the Parc de Procé.

I now recall Robert Desnos, in the period that those of us who experienced it call the *sleeping fits*. He's "asleep," but writing, talking. It's evening, my home, in the studio above the cabaret Le Ciel. Outside, someone is shouting, "Come one, come all, into the Chat Noir!" And Desnos keeps seeing what I cannot see, what I see only as he gradually reveals it to me. He borrows the personality of the rarest, most ungraspable, most disappointing man alive, the creator of *Cemetery of Uniforms and Liveries*: Marcel Duchamp. The two have never met in real life. What seemed most inimitable about Duchamp, his mysterious "word games" (Rrose Sélavy), resurfaces in all its purity in Desnos and suddenly takes on extraordinary breadth. Whoever hasn't seen his pencil trace those astonishing poetic equations, with prodigious speed and without the slightest hesitation, and who hasn't been able to verify, as I have, that they could not have been composed in advance—even while appreciating their technical perfection and their marvelous audacity—cannot conceive of what this meant back then, the absolute oracular value it assumed. Someone who was present at those countless sessions should undertake to describe them dispassionately and precisely, situate them in their true atmosphere.

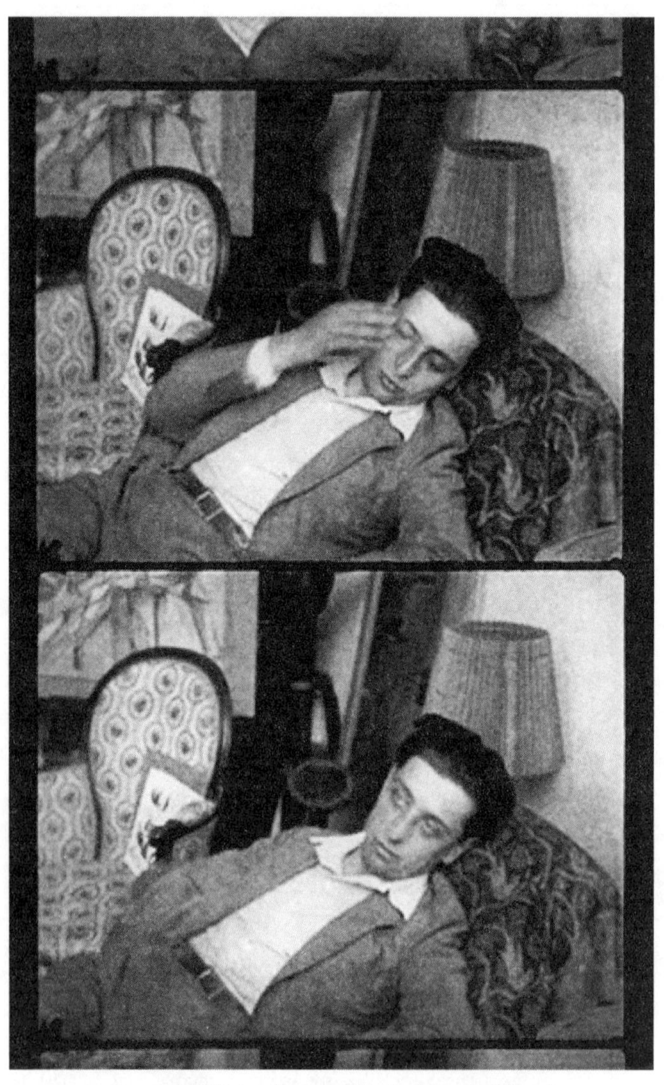

I now recall Robert Desnos (Film by Man Ray) (p. 19)

The topic calls for a thorough discussion. Of the many rendezvous that Desnos, with eyes closed, set for me for later on—with him, with someone else, or with myself—even now there is not one I would dare miss; not one, no matter how implausible the time and place, where I wouldn't be certain of finding the person he predicted.

Meanwhile, you can be sure of running into me in Paris, of spending no more than three days without seeing me come and go on boulevard Bonne-Nouvelle, in late afternoon, between the *Matin* printing plant and boulevard de Strasbourg. I don't know why it's there, in fact, that my steps always lead me, that I almost always end up with no particular goal, with no determining factor other than the obscure conviction that this is where it (?) will occur. I can hardly see, on this brief stroll, what could possibly be a center of attraction for me here, not even one I don't yet know, in space or time. No, not even the very beautiful and very useless Porte Saint-Denis. Not even the memory of the eighth and final episode of a film I saw in that neighborhood, in which a Chinese man, who had found some mysterious method of multiplying himself, invaded New York on his own, in several million copies of himself alone. He strode, followed by himself, and himself, and himself, and himself, into the office of President Wilson, who removed his pince-nez. This film, by far the most striking I've ever seen, was called *The Trail of the Octopus*.

My habit of never consulting the program before going into a cinema—which in any case would get me nowhere, since I've never been able to retain the names of more than five or

No, not even the very beautiful and very useless Porte Saint-Denis . . . (p. 21)

Cie Gle FRANÇAISE DE CINÉMATOGRAPHIE

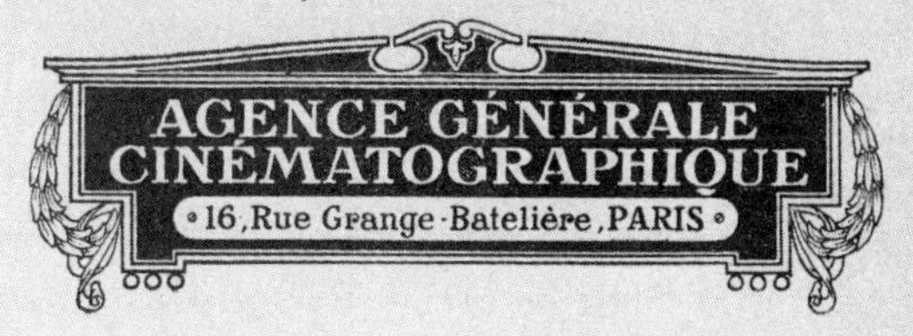

L'Étreinte de la Pieuvre

Grand Sérial mystérieux en 15 épisodes,
Interprété par Ben Wilson et Neva Gerber.

Cinquième épisode : L'Œil de Satan

Quelle situation épouvantable que celle de Ruth et de Carter entraînés tous deux dans le wagon détaché du train vers l'abîme ! Le pont mobile est ouvert, la voiture qui enferme les deux jeunes gens va se trouver précipitée dans le fleuve. Heureusement, Carter arrive à manœuvrer le frein de la voiture : une fraction de seconde plus tard, et elle plongeait dans les flots.

Mais les Zélateurs de Satan guettaient. Leur ruse infernale ayant échoué, ils se ruent sur Carter : il est jeté dans le fleuve. Quant à Ruth, elle est ligotée, bâillonnée et emmenée en automobile à San Francisco, chez Hop Lee, émissaire du Dr Wang Foo.

Carter est un intrépide nageur. Il arrive à remonter à la surface des eaux, à revenir sur la berge, et la Providence fait que son fidèle lieutenant Sandy Mac Nab, auquel il avait donné l'ordre de le suivre en automobile, apparaît et l'aide à monter dans la voiture. Carter et Sandy filent à toute allure vers San Francisco.

Là, Carter débarque à l'hôtel Wellington ou les Zélateurs de Satan ont tôt fait de le dépister. Lui ne songe qu'à retrouver Ruth. Or, dans l'hôtel, il rencontre Jean Al Kasim qui lui donne un renseignement précieux : Mme Zora, la femme qui voulait tuer Ruth, se trouve logée justement dans la chambre voisine de celle de Carter. Peut-être, en surprenant une conversation de cette femme avec ses complices, Carter arrivera-t-il à découvrir la retraite de Ruth. Carter écoute. Il apprend que la jeune fille est cachée dans le quartier chinois. Il surprend le mot de passe des conjurés, qui est : « L'Œil de Satan. » Il s'est procuré un masque noir identique à celui de L'Homme au Masque, et il pourrait, en passant pour ce dernier, sauver la jeune fille, s'il connaissait plus précisément la place où elle est séquestrée.

Mais il faut commencer les recherches. Carter se rend au bureau du chef de la police. Là un étrange appel téléphonique lui révèle ce qu'il désirait tant savoir. En effet, Ruth Stanhope, qui est entre les mains de Hop Lee, a usé d'un habile stratagème : sans éveiller l'attention de son gardien, elle a soulevé le récepteur de l'appareil et demandé la communication avec le bureau de la police, et c'est elle-même qui, au téléphone, révèle à

This film, by far the most striking I've ever seen (p. 21)

six actors—obviously puts me at risk of being "unluckier" than the average viewer, even though I must confess here my weakness for the most idiotic French films. Moreover, I *understand* very little, I *follow* too loosely. Sometimes it ends up bothering me, at which point I question those sitting next to me. Be that as it may, certain movie houses in the tenth arrondissement seem particularly suitable places for me to go, as in the days when Jacques Vaché and I, in the stalls of the old Folies-Dramatiques, would settle in for dinner, opening cans, slicing bread, uncorking bottles, and speaking at full volume as if at a table, to the stupefaction of the moviegoers, who didn't dare say a word.

In this regard, the Théâtre Moderne, located at the end of the now demolished Passage de l'Opéra, apart from the fact that the plays they put on were even less noteworthy than those films, responded perfectly to my ideal. The mediocre performances of the actors, who paid scant attention to their roles, barely listening to one another and busy making dates with the audience, which comprised at most fifteen persons, never struck me as more than a backdrop. But what could better suit this fugitive and easily *alerted* image of myself, the one I've been talking about, than the lobby of that theater, with its tall, worn mirrors, decorated at the base with gray swans gliding through yellow reeds, and its dark, airless, unnerving grillwork loges; than that auditorium, where during the performance rats scurried over your feet, and where you had the choice, on entering, between a staved-in chair and one that tipped over backward! And honestly, what will I ever see, between the first and second acts (no point expecting a third), to match the equally crepuscular

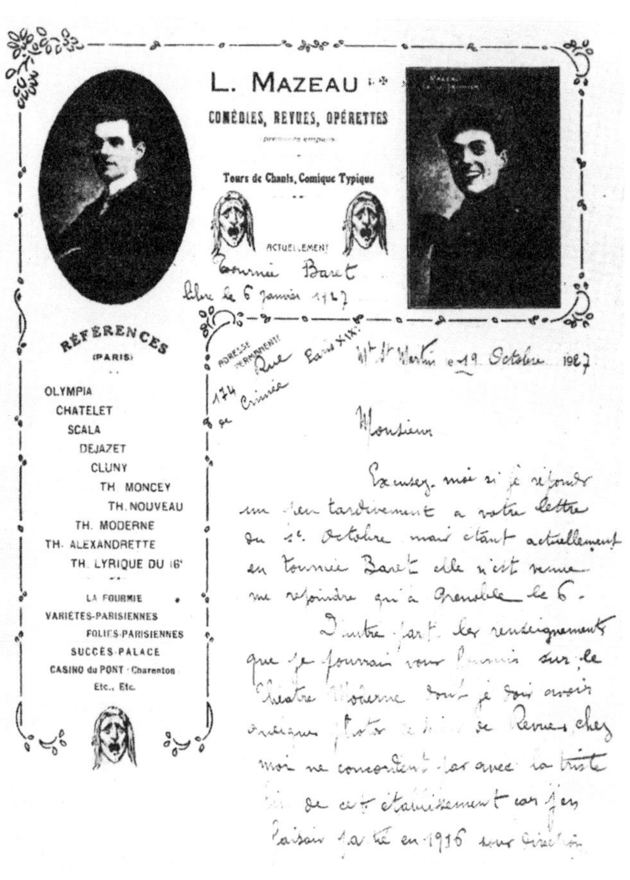

L. MAZEAU

COMÉDIES, REVUES, OPÉRETTES

Tours de Chants, Comique Typique

ACTUELLEMENT
Tournée Baret
Libre le 6 Janvier 1927

RÉFÉRENCES
(PARIS)

OLYMPIA
CHATELET
SCALA
DEJAZET
CLUNY
TH. MONCEY
TH. NOUVEAU
TH. MODERNE
TH. ALEXANDRETTE
TH. LYRIQUE DU 16e

LA FOURMIE
VARIÉTÉS-PARISIENNES
FOLIES-PARISIENNES
SUCCÈS-PALACE
CASINO du PONT - Charenton
Etc., Etc.

ADRESSE PERMANENTE 174 Rue de Crimée Paris XIXe

Mt St Martin le 19 Octobre 1927

Monsieur

Excusez-moi si je réponds un peu tardivement à votre lettre du 1er Octobre mais étant actuellement en tournée Baret elle n'est venue me rejoindre qu'à Grenoble le 6.

D'autre part les renseignements que je pourrai vous fournir sur le Théâtre Moderne dont je dois avoir quelques photos de Revues chez moi ne concordent pas avec la triste [illegible] de cet établissement car j'en faisais partie en 1916 sous direction

Concerning the Théâtre Moderne (p. 24)

de Monsieur Julien non comme Régisseur qui était
alors Monsieur St Bonnet mais comme artiste
et je vous prie de croire que le travail que l'on y
faisait et propre et intensif et quoique les spectacles
fussent toujours lestes la morale dans l'intérieur de la
maison y fut toujours maintenu exemplaire grâce a la
poigne de son excellent directeur évidemment ont ne pourrait
en dire autant sous la Direction Choppi qui fit crouler
la maison. Quoique il en soit ne croyez-vous pas cher
Monsieur si comme je le pense vous avez et je vous le souhaite
~~[illegible]~~ l'esprit necessaire pour faire un volume sur les
theatres, le faire sur les grands et non sur les petits. laissons
ses derniers dans leur pourriture plaignons les pauvres artistes
qui sont obligés d'y séjourner quelque temps pour gagner
leur vie et ne montrons pas a quelques lecteurs aguichés
par un titre ronflant les dessous ou les coulisses de 2 ou 3
établissements de Paris qui s'intitulent theatres et dont vos quelques
lecteurs verraient encore la généralité de notre corporation
qui fait tout ce quelle peut pour se sortir d'une morale
fausse que lui fait encore un public vicieux frequentant
les théatres dont vous voulez tracer quelques scènes (ils ne valent
ni l'encre ni le temps qu'on y perdrait pour eux. faisons plutot
une guerre acharnée [illegible] ..... Directeurs ou Directrices ..... mais
autrement que par écrit. ne remuons pas trop la poubelle elle
sent mauvais et nous avons créé l'Union des Artistes
pour [illegible] les camarades obligés de séjourner dans ces
bouges. Conclusion ne comptez sur aucun renseignements de ma
part je n'ai connu le Moderne qu'en 1916-1917 - je n'y suis jamais

été Régisseur et je vous prie de croire que je ne perdrai jamais mon [illegible] à lire votre
..... ouvrage ..... si réellement [illegible] s'il y a tant de belles choses à lire ..... Souhaitant [illegible]
[illegible] Veuillez croire cher Monsieur à mes bien [illegible]

Concerning the Théâtre Moderne (p. 24)

"bar" upstairs, with its impenetrable tunnels—a veritable "salon at the bottom of a lake"? Having been there many times, I've taken away, at the cost of some truly unimaginable horrors, the memory of a perfectly pure quatrain, sung by an extraordinarily pretty woman:

> Ready is my heart's abode,
> The future it welcomes eagerly.
> Since there's nothing I repent,
> Handsome husband, come to me.*

I've always felt an incredibly strong desire to meet, in the woods at night, a beautiful naked woman—or rather, since such a desire, once expressed, loses its meaning, I feel an incredibly strong regret at never having met her. After all, it's not so crazy to imagine such an encounter: it could happen. It seems to me that *everything* would stop dead, and I would not be writing what I'm writing. I adore such a situation, which more than any other would likely obliterate my *presence of mind*. I doubt I'd even think to run away. (Anyone who laughs at that last sentence is a pig.) One late afternoon last year, in the gallerias around the Electric-Palace cinema, a very pale nude woman, who would have needed only to shrug off her coat, was indeed wandering from row to row. It was deeply moving in itself but, sadly, far from extraordinary, as that corner of the Electric-Palace is a common site for assignations.

But to really descend into the lower depths of the mind, where it is no longer about night falling or rising (is it really

*Variant: "My new lover, come to me."

daylight out?), I'd have to come back to rue Fontaine, to the Théâtre des Deux-Masques, which has now been replaced by a cabaret. I went there once, I who never attend the theater, on the assurance that the play they were performing had to be watchable, given how rabidly the critics had gone after it, even demanding it be banned. Amid the Grand Guignol–type melodramas that were the theater's bread and butter, this one felt seriously out of place—not a bad recommendation. I won't delay in expressing my boundless admiration for *The Deranged*, which remains and will long remain the only dramatic work (by which I mean, written specifically for the stage) that I care to remember. I emphasize that the play, and this is not its least peculiar aspect, loses almost all its effect if it isn't *seen*, or at least if each character's lines aren't acted out. Those reservations aside, it seems worthwhile to summarize the plot.

The curtain rises on the principal's office in a girls' boarding school. The principal, a corpulent blond in her forties, is alone and shows signs of great agitation. It's the eve of the school holidays, and she's anxiously awaiting someone's arrival: "Solange should be here by now..." She paces restlessly around the room, touching the furniture, the papers on her desk. Now and again she goes to the window that looks out on the grounds, where recess has just begun. We have heard the bell ring, then the joyful shouts of little girls, which are immediately absorbed into the distant hubbub. A dull-witted gardener—the school's gardener—who nods his head and speaks with intolerable slowness, with huge delays in comprehension and faulty pronunciation, now stands in the doorway, mumbling vague words and apparently not about to go away. He has just come back from the station, where he didn't see Miss Solange get off the train:

"Miiiss-So-laaan-ge..." He drags his syllables like feet. We, too, grow impatient. Meanwhile, an elderly dowager, who has just handed over her calling card, is ushered in. Her granddaughter has sent her a rather confused letter in which she begs to be taken home right away. The old woman easily lets herself be mollified: at this time of year, the children are always a bit nervous. Besides, we need only call in the little one to ask whether she has any complaints about anyone or anything. Here she is. She kisses her grandmother. Soon we see that she can no longer tear her eyes away from those of the woman questioning her. She limits herself to a few gestures of denial. Why not wait for the scholastic prize ceremony, which is only a few days away? We can tell that she doesn't dare say anything. She'll stay. The child starts to exit, subdued. She moves toward the door. On the threshold, she seems to be suffering a great inner conflict. She runs out. The grandmother takes her leave, with profuse thanks. Again the principal is alone. The absurd, terrible wait, when you don't know which object to move, which movement to repeat, what to do to make the anticipated thing arrive... Finally, the sound of a car engine... The principal's eyes light up. Facing eternity. A lovely woman enters without knocking. It's she. She gently pushes away the arms embracing her. Hair brown or chestnut, I'm not sure. Young. Magnificent eyes filled with languor, despair, shrewdness, cruelty. Slim, soberly clad, a dark-colored dress, black silk stockings. And that hint of "déclassé" that we so relish. No explanation of why she's here, she apologizes for having been held up. Her sheer, evident coldness contrasts starkly with the welcome she's offered. She speaks, with an indifference that sounds affected, about what her life has been like, not much happening since she was last here, at around the same time the year before.

No details about the school where she teaches. But (*here the conversation takes an infinitely more intimate turn*) it now concerns the privileged relations Solange has had with certain pupils who were more charming than the others, prettier, smarter. She grows dreamy. Her words fade into a murmur. Suddenly she stops short, we see her open her handbag and, uncovering a marvelous thigh, there, slightly above her dark garter... "But, you never used to shoot up!"—"No, oh, these days, what can you do." The reply given in a tone so poignantly weary. As if reanimated, Solange inquires in turn: "And what about you, and this place? Tell me everything." Here, too, there are some *new* pupils who are very nice. One in particular. So sweet. "Come, darling, look." The two women lean for a long time at the window. Silence. A BALL FALLS INTO THE ROOM. Silence. "That's the one! She's going to come up."—"You think so?" Both standing, leaning against the wall. Solange closes her eyes, relaxes, sighs, stands still. A knock. The child from before enters without saying a word, heads slowly toward the ball, her eyes riveted on the principal's; she walks on tiptoe. Curtain.—The next act opens at night in an anteroom. Several hours have passed. A doctor, with his bag. One of the children has disappeared. Let's hope nothing bad has happened to her! Everyone is rushing around, the house and grounds have been searched top to bottom. The principal, calmer than before. "A very sweet child, maybe a little sad. Heavens, and her grandmother was right here only a few hours ago! I've sent for her." The suspicious doctor: two years in a row, an accident just before the pupils leave on holiday. Last year, the child's body discovered in the well. This year... The bleating, blustery gardener. He has gone to check the well. "It's a queer thing; talk about something queer, that's queer."

The child from before enters without saying a word . . .
(Photo by Henri Manuel) (p. 30)

The doctor questions the gardener, in vain: "It's queer." He has searched all over the grounds with his lantern. And the little girl couldn't possibly have gotten out. Doors locked. Walls too high. No trace of her anywhere in the house. The brute continues to quibble miserably with himself, churning over the same things, less and less intelligibly. The doctor has stopped paying attention. "It's a queer thing. Just like last year. Didn't see nothing myself. Tomorrow gotta put out another candle...Where could that littl'un be? Doctor? Oh, well, doctor. Still, it's queer... And just when Miiiss-So-laaange arrived yesterday afternoon and..."—"Wait, did you say Miss Solange is here? Are you sure? (Ah! It's more like last year than I thought!) Leave me now." The doctor lies in wait behind a column. It's not yet dawn. Solange crosses the stage. She does not seem to be sharing in the general agitation but walks straight ahead like an automaton.—A little later. Every search has been in vain. We're back in the principal's office. The child's grandmother has just fainted in the parlor. She must be attended to right away. The two women plainly seem to have nothing on their conscience. We look at the doctor. The police commissioner. The servants. Solange. The principal...The latter, going to fetch a cordial, walks to the medicine cabinet, opens it. The bloody corpse of the little girl tumbles out, head first, and collapses onto the floor. The scream, the unforgettable scream. (At the performance, they'd deemed it wise to alert the public that the actress playing the child was over seventeen. The main thing was that she looked eleven.) I don't know if the scream I mentioned was the actual end of the play, but I hope its authors (it was a collaborative effort between the comic actor Palau and, I believe, a surgeon named Thierry—as well as some demon, no doubt) did not intend for Solange to be harassed any further or that this character, too tempting to be true, should have to suffer a semblance of punishment that, moreover, she negated in all her splendor. I'll add merely that the part was played by the most admirable and no doubt the *only* actress of our times, whom I've seen in several other plays at the Deux-Masques, in which she was no less beautiful, but about whom, perhaps to my great shame, I've heard nothing further: Blanche Derval.

(Finishing the preceding account last night, I again drifted into the sorts of musings that have occurred to me every time I've seen that play—in other words, two or three times—or when I've run through it in my head. The lack of sufficient clues about what happens after the ball falls, about what has taken hold of Solange and her partner to make them such superb beasts of prey, remains utterly confounding. On waking this morning, I had more difficulty than usual ridding myself of a fairly vile dream that I don't feel it necessary to transcribe here, as it derived in large part from conversations I had yesterday, completely unrelated to the matter at hand. The dream seemed interesting insofar as it was symptomatic of the repercussions that such memories can have on the course of one's thinking, if one violently abandons oneself to them. First, it is remarkable to note that this dream brought out only the painful, repugnant, even heinous side of the matters I'd been pondering, that it scrupulously concealed anything that normally I would consider their fabulous prize, like an extract of amber or attar of roses from across the centuries. Moreover, we must admit that if I wake up and see with extreme lucidity what has just occurred—a moss-colored insect nearly two feet in length, having substituted itself for an old man, headed toward a kind of slot machine and dropped one coin into the slot instead of two,

Blanche Derval (Photo by Henri Manuel) (p. 33)

which to me seemed such a reprehensible act of fraud that, as if accidentally, I struck it with my cane and felt it jump on my head: I just had time to notice the orbs of its eyes shine on the brim of my hat before I began suffocating, and only with great difficulty was someone able to disengage two of its large hairy legs from my throat, while I felt an indescribable revulsion—it is clear that, on a superficial level, this is *especially* related to the fact that under the eaves of the loggia where I've been staying these past few days is a nest, around which a bird is fluttering, clearly alarmed by my presence, and that each time it returns squawking from the fields, it brings back something like a fat green grasshopper. Still, there's no denying that the transposition, the intense fixation, the otherwise inexplicable passage of this type of image from the register of mere observation to that of emotion, is mainly due to the evocation of certain episodes from *The Deranged* and my return to those musings I mentioned. Since the production of dream imagery always requires at least this *double play of mirrors*, it indicates the highly special, no doubt eminently revelatory, and exceedingly "overdetermined" role—in the Freudian sense—that certain powerful impressions, uncontaminated by morality, are called upon to play, and that are experienced as "beyond good and evil" in dreams and, subsequently, in what we arbitrarily oppose to them under the name of reality.)

The very great, very keen emotion that reading Rimbaud aroused in me around 1915, and that I now get from only a handful of his poems, such as "Devotion," is no doubt what caused me, one day around that time, as I was out alone in a provincial town under the driving rain, to meet a girl who came up to me and, without preamble, as we walked a few steps together, asked my permission to recite one of her favorite poems, "Sleeper in the Valley." It was so unexpected, so out of season. Just recently again, when one Sunday while at the Saint-Ouen flea market with Marcel Noll (I often go there in search of objects you can't find anywhere else: outmoded, broken, unusable, almost incomprehensible, and ultimately perverse in the sense I understand and love—for instance, a kind of shellacked, irregular white semicylinder, with reliefs and depressions that make no sense to me, and with horizontal and vertical red and green lines, carefully housed in a special case and bearing an inscription in Italian, which I brought home and which, after a thorough examination, I concluded was no more than the three-dimensional statistical model of a city's population between two given years, none of which made it any more intelligible), our attention was drawn simultaneously to a brand-new copy of Rimbaud's *Complete Works*, buried in a very small and meager heap of rags, yellowed photographs from the previous century, worthless books, and tin spoons. Luckily I decided to leaf through it, as I discovered two inserted sheets of paper: a typescript of a poem in free verse, and notes and reflections in pencil concerning Nietzsche. But the seller didn't give me time to learn more. The book is not for sale, the documents in it are hers. She's very young and quite jovial. She continues to speak animatedly to someone she knows who appears to be a laborer and who seems to be listening to her with rapt attention. Then we engage her in conversation. She's cultured, gladly tells us about her literary likes, which are Shelley, Nietzsche, and Rimbaud. She even begins talking unprompted about the Surrealists, and about *Paris Peasant* by Louis Aragon, which she couldn't read to

One Sunday while at the Saint-Ouen flea market . . . (p. 36)

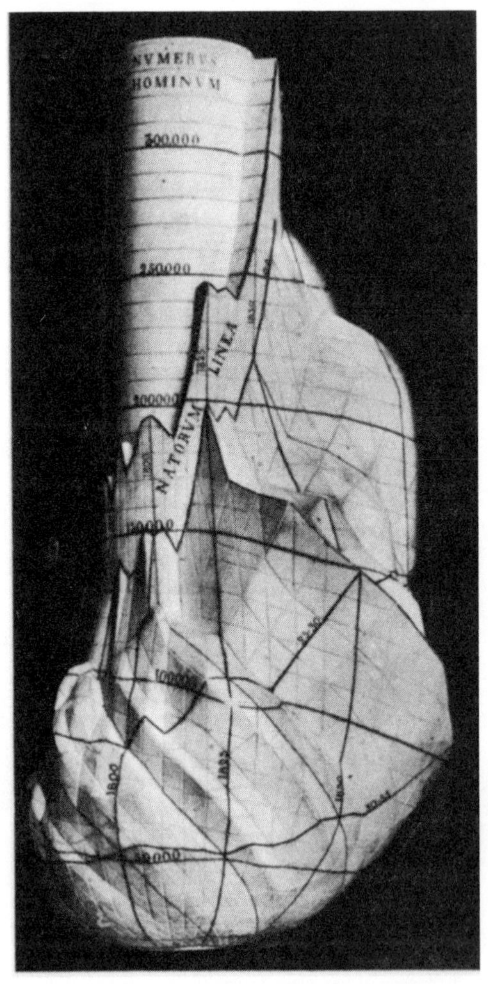

Perverse . . . a kind of shellacked, irregular
white semicylinder . . . (p. 36)

the end, having been put off by the variations on the word *Pessimism*. Everything she says demonstrates great faith in the Revolution. At my request, she gives me her poem that I had found in the book, along with several others, all of them interesting. Her name is Fanny Beznos.

I also recall the supposedly jocular proposal made to a lady one day in my presence, that she bequeath to the Surrealist Central one of the astounding sky-blue gloves she had put on to visit us there, the fear that gripped me at seeing her acquiesce, and my beseeching her not to do anything of the kind. I don't know what I could have found at that moment so terrifyingly, so marvelously decisive about the thought of that glove leaving that hand forever. Even so, it did not take on its true, larger proportions, by which I mean the ones it still has, until the moment when that lady promised to return and place on the table, at the precise spot where I had ardently hoped she would not leave her blue glove, another glove made of bronze that she owns and that I've since seen at her home—also a woman's glove, folded at the wrist, its fingers flat; a glove that I've never been able to resist picking up, each time surprised by how heavy it is, and apparently wishing only to measure its exact weight at the spot where the other would have weighed nothing at all.

Just a few days ago, Louis Aragon pointed out to me that the sign on a hotel in Pourville, which bears in red letters the words MAISON ROUGE, was written in such a style and arranged in such a way that, at a certain oblique angle from the road, MAISON disappeared and ROUGE could be read

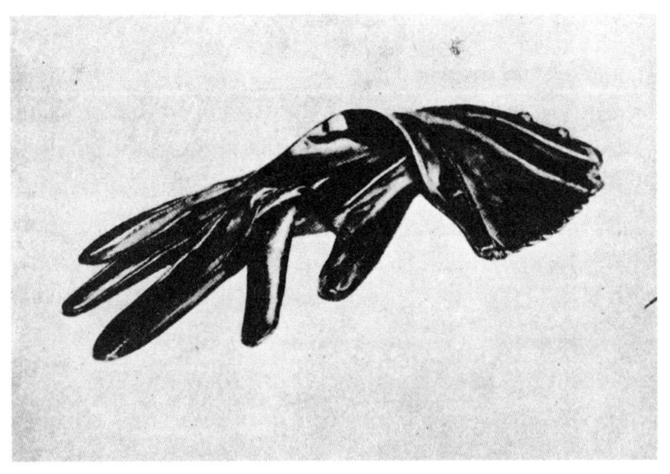

Also a woman's glove . . . (p. 39)

as POLICE. This optical illusion would be insignificant were it not for the fact that on the same day, an hour or two later, the woman we called *the lady of the glove* showed me a trompe l'oeil picture such as I'd never seen, which came with the house she had recently rented. It's an antique engraving that, when viewed head-on, depicts a tiger, but is stratified vertically by thin strips that divide up another image: if you step back to the left, a vase; step back to the right, an angel. I'm highlighting these two facts because, to my mind, under those conditions, their juxtaposition was inevitable and because it seems to me singularly impossible to establish a rational correlation between the two.

I hope, in any case, that the presentation of these dozen observations and of the one that follows will be of a nature to drive some people out into the street, having made them realize the uselessness, or at least the grave inadequacy, of any supposedly rigorous self-reckoning, of any action that demands sustained concentration or that might have been premeditated. The slightest occurrence, if it is truly unforeseen, scatters everything to the wind. And after this, let no one speak to me about work, I mean about the moral value of work. I am forced to accept the idea of work as a material necessity, and as such I completely support it being shared in the best, in other words the most equitable, way. That the sinister obligations of my life impose work on me, so be it; that anyone ask me to believe in it, to revere my or others' labor, never. I prefer, once again, to walk in darkness while believing I'm walking in daylight. There is no point in being alive if you have to work. The event from which each of us is entitled to expect the revelation of our life's meaning, the event that I might not yet have encountered, but on the road to which I seek myself, *is not to be earned by work*. But I'm getting ahead of myself, for perhaps it was this above all that let me understand at the time, and that now justifies without further delay, Nadja's appearance on the scene.

And finally the tower of the Manoir d'Ango blows sky high, and a blizzard of feathers, falling from the dovecote, melts upon touching the ground of the huge courtyard that was once paved with remnants of tile and is now covered in real blood!

LAST OCTOBER 4, at the end of one of those completely idle and dreary afternoons that I have a knack for spending, I found myself on rue Lafayette. After pausing for a moment at the stall outside the *Humanité* bookshop and buying Trotsky's latest volume, I pushed on aimlessly toward the Opéra. The offices and shops were starting to empty, the doors of buildings up and down the street were closing, people on the sidewalks were taking their leave, and it was growing more crowded. Somewhat unconsciously, I studied the faces, the clothes, the bearings: it was not yet *these* folks who would wage the Revolution. I had just crossed the intersection whose name I don't know, in front of a church. Suddenly, when she is still perhaps ten paces from me, coming in the opposite direction, I see a young woman, very poorly dressed, who also sees me or had seen me. She walks with head held high, unlike all the other pedestrians. So slight that her feet barely touch the ground. An imperceptible smile might be playing about her lips. Curiously made up, like someone who, having begun with the eyes, didn't have time to finish, leaving the rims of those eyes so dark for a blond. The rims, not the lids. (Such a dazzling effect can be obtained, and obtained only, if you carefully run the eyeliner pencil under the lid, at the waterline. It is interesting to note in this regard that Blanche Derval in the role of

The *Humanité* bookshop (p. 43)

Solange, even seen from up close, did not appear to be wearing makeup. Does this mean that I value what is barely tolerated in the street but recommended in the theater only if one disregards its being forbidden in one case and mandatory in the other? Perhaps.) I had never seen such eyes. Without a moment's hesitation, I speak to the stranger, all the while, I freely admit, expecting the worst. She smiles, but very mysteriously, and, I would say, "*knowingly*," even though I wouldn't have thought so at the time. She claims to be going to a hairdresser's on boulevard Magenta (I say "claims" because she later admitted she wasn't going anywhere). She tells me somewhat insistently about the difficulties she's having with money but mainly, it seems, as an excuse and explanation for the considerable shabbiness of her outfit. We stop at a café near the Gare du Nord.

I look at her more closely. What can be going on in those eyes that is so extraordinary? What is reflected in them, that mix of obscure distress and luminous pride? This is also the enigma posed by the confession she starts making to me, without asking for anything more, with a confidence that might (or might not?) be misplaced. In Lille, the city she comes from and that she left only two or three years before, she knew a student who loved her and whom she might have loved. One day, she decided to leave him when he least expected it, "so as not to hold him back." That's when she came to Paris, from where she wrote to him at longer and longer intervals without ever giving out her address. Nevertheless, about a year later they ran into each other here in the city, to their mutual surprise. Taking her hands, he couldn't help saying how much she had changed and, staring at those hands, he was amazed to see how well manicured they were (they aren't now). Then mechanically, in turn, she looked at one of the hands that were holding hers and couldn't repress a cry when she noticed that the last two fingers were fused together. "You've been injured!" The young man was forced to show her his other hand, which presented the same deformity. She questions me about this at length, with great feeling: "Is that possible? To have lived so long with someone, had every possible opportunity to observe him, to make a point of discovering every one of his physical and other peculiarities, and still know so little about him, still not even notice *that*! Do you think, do you think love can do such things? And he was so angry, what can you expect, all I could do at that point was keep my mouth shut—those hands... Then he said something I don't understand, a word I don't understand, he said: 'You mooncalf! I'm going back to Alsace-Lorraine. Over there, women know how to love.' Why 'mooncalf'? Do you know?" Naturally, I react rather strongly to the statement she has just quoted. "No matter. But I find those generalities about Alsace-Lorraine odious, this individual is certainly an utter cretin, etc.... So, he's gone, and you haven't seen him since? So much the better." She tells me her name, the one she's chosen for herself: "Nadja, because in Russian it's the beginning of the word for hope, and because it's only the beginning."

Only now does she think to ask me who I am (in the very limited sense of the word). I tell her. Then she goes back to her past, talks about her parents. She is especially moved by the memory of her father: "Such a weak man! If you knew how weak he's always been. When he was young, you see, they never refused him anything. His parents, very well off. There weren't cars yet, but even so, a fine carriage, a coachman... He frittered it all away. I love him so much. Whenever I think of him, when I tell myself just how weak he is...

Oh, it's not the same with Mother. She's a good woman, as people say, a *fine* woman. Not at all the wife my father should have had. At our house, everything was spic-and-span, of course, but, you understand, he wasn't the type who liked to come home and see her in an apron. It's true he found his table all set, dinner ready to serve, but he didn't find what they call" (with an ironically greedy expression and an amusing gesture) "a lavish 'spread.' I'm very fond of Mother, I wouldn't want to hurt her for the world. So when I came to Paris, I told her I had a letter of reference to the Vaugirard convent. Naturally I never used it. But when I write to her, I always end my letter by saying: 'I hope to see you soon,' and I add: 'God willing, as Sister So-and-So says'... I make up a name. How happy that must make her! In her letters to me, what touches me most, what I'd give all the rest for, are the postscripts. She always feels compelled to add: 'I wonder what you could be doing in Paris.' Poor Mother, if she only knew!"

What Nadja is doing in Paris, she herself wonders as well. In the evening, at around seven, she likes to be in a second-class car of the metro. Most of the riders are people who have finished work. She sits among them, tries to guess from their faces what could be occupying their thoughts. No doubt they're fretting about what they've left undone until tomorrow, only until tomorrow, or what's awaiting them that evening, which cheers them up or makes them more anxious. Nadja stares into space: "Those are some decent people." More agitated than I wish to appear, this time I get angry: "Hardly! Anyway, it's not about that. Those people can't be interesting as long as they can stand working for a living, no matter what other cares they have. How can this elevate them if their strongest impulse isn't revolt? Besides, at that moment, you see them but they don't see you. Personally, I hate with all my might the servitude that everyone wants me to uphold. I pity people for being condemned to it, for not being able to escape it, but it's not the hardships they endure that will make me feel kindly toward them; it is, and could only be, the vigor of their protest. I know that people can still feel free even at a factory furnace, or at one of those machines that inexorably force you, day in and day out, to make the same repetitive movement every few seconds, or when subject to intolerable orders, or in a cell, or before a firing squad, but it's not the torture they suffer that confers this freedom. It is, I fully believe this, a perpetual unshackling—and even then, this unshackling becomes possible, constantly possible, only if those shackles do not crush us, as they do so many of those you're talking about. But it is also, and perhaps even more so in human terms, the relatively long but marvelous line of footsteps that a man can follow when unchained. Do you think they're capable of taking those steps? Do they even have the time? Do they have the courage? Decent people, you said: yes, decent, like the ones who get themselves killed in wartime, right? The point is this: heroes are a bunch of unfortunate wretches and a few poor imbeciles. Personally, I confess that those *steps* are all that matters. Where are they going, that's the real question. They'll surely end up forging a path, and who knows whether on that path it will become clear how to loosen your chains, or to help loosen the chains of those who couldn't follow it. Only then will it be all right to pause for a moment, but without ever going backward." (You get an idea of what I can say on the subject, provided I remember to treat it concretely.)

Nadja listens and doesn't try to contradict me. Perhaps she only meant to praise the notion of work. She starts telling me about her health, which is very precarious. The doctor she consulted, whom she'd chosen because she felt she could trust him, ordered an immediate cure, for all the money she had left, at the Mont-Doré spa. The idea delights her, given how impracticable such a trip would be. Instead, she has decided that steady manual labor could make up for this unfeasible cure. And so she applied for work in a bakery or butcher shop, where, her purely poetic judgment told her, she had the greatest chances of staying healthy. Each time, she was offered a paltry salary. Sometimes, before answering, they gave her the once-over. One baker, who had promised her seventeen francs a day, checked her out, then corrected himself: seventeen or eighteen. Very cheerfully: "I told him, seventeen, it's a deal; eighteen, no."

We are now walking along a narrow street, I think rue du Faubourg-Poissonnière. It's dinnertime. I start to take my leave. She asks who's expecting me. "My wife."—"Married! Oh! Well, then..." And in another tone, very serious and contemplative: "Too bad. But... and that grand idea of yours? I was beginning to see it so clearly. It truly is a star, a star toward which you were heading. You cannot fail to reach that star. Hearing you talk, I felt that nothing would prevent you—nothing, not even me... You can never see that star as I saw it. You don't understand: it's like the heart of a heartless flower." I am very moved. To change the subject, I ask where she's planning to have dinner. And suddenly that lightness that I've seen only in her, perhaps indeed that *freedom*: "Where?" Her finger points. "Well, there, or there" (the two closest restaurants), "where I am, of course. It's always that way." Before leaving, I want to ask her a question that would sum up all the others, a question that probably only I would ever ask but that has at least once received a worthy reply: "Who are you?" And she, without missing a beat: "I am the wandering soul." We part company, agreeing to meet the next day at the bar on the corner of rue Lafayette and Faubourg-Poissonnière. She makes me promise to bring some of my books, even though I strongly advise her against reading them. Life is other than what one writes. Then she holds me back a few moments longer to tell me what touches her about me. It is, in my thinking, my language, my entire way of being, it seems—and this is one of the compliments that has most affected me—my *simplicity*.

October 5.—Nadja has arrived first, ahead of time. She's no longer the same as yesterday. Rather elegant, dressed entirely in black and red, a very pretty hat that she takes off, revealing her straw-colored hair that has given up its incredible disorder, silk stockings, shoes that are, unlike the first pair, very suitable. Our conversation has also become more constrained and begins, on her part, somewhat haltingly. That is, until she picks up the books I've brought for her (*The Lost Steps, Manifesto of Surrealism*): "Lost steps! But there aren't any." She leafs through the book with great curiosity. Her attention is drawn to a poem I've quoted by Jarry:

> The pubic arch of menhirs straddles the moor...

Instead of putting her off, this poem, which she reads once fairly quickly, then studies more carefully, seems to have a profound effect on her. At the end of the second quatrain, her eyes tear up and are filled with the vision of a forest. She sees the poet passing near that forest, as if she's following him from a distance: "No, he's skirting the forest. He cannot enter, he doesn't go in." Then she loses him and returns to the poem, a little before where she left off, asking about the words that surprise her most, giving each one the sign of complicity or precise assent that it requires.

Hunts with their steel the marten and ermine.

With their steel? The marten ... and ermine. Yes, I see: the frigid hollows, the ice-cold rivers: *with their steel.* A bit farther down:

C'havann, the owl, eating the whirr of maybugs,

(In fright, shutting the book:) "Oh! That's death!"

The color relationship between the covers of the two books surprises and seduces her. Apparently it "suits" me. I've surely done it on purpose (which is true). Then she tells me about two friends she had. One, upon her arrival in Paris, whom she habitually refers to as "Special Friend"; that was what she called him because he never wanted her to know who he was. She still feels great veneration for him, a man of around seventy-five, who had spent years in the colonies, and who told her when he left that he was returning to Senegal. The other, an American, who seems to have inspired very different feelings in her: "And besides, he called me Lena, in memory of his dead daughter. It's very affectionate, very touching, don't you think? Sometimes I could no longer stand being called that, as if in a dream: Lena, Lena ... So I would wave my hand in front of his eyes, like this, and say: No, not Lena, Nadja." We go out. She continues: "I see your home. Your wife. Brunette, of course. Small. Pretty. And next to her is a dog. Maybe also, but somewhere else, a cat" (all true). "For the moment, that's all I see." I'm about to go home; Nadja accompanies me in a taxi. We remain silent for a while, then abruptly she starts using the familiar *tu* with me: "A game: say something. Anything, a number, a name. Like this" (she closes her eyes): "Two, two what? Two women. What do these women look like? Dressed in black. Where are they? In a park. And what are they doing?... Oh, come on, it's so easy, why don't you want to play? Anyway, that's how I talk to myself when I'm alone; I tell myself all kinds of stories. And not only stories: that's pretty much how I live all the time."* I leave her at my door: "And what will I do now? Where will I go? But it's so simple to head slowly back toward rue Lafayette, Faubourg-Poissonnière, to start by returning to exactly where we were."

October 6.—To avoid loitering too much, I leave home at around four, intending to go on foot to the Nouvelle France, where Nadja is supposed to meet me at five-thirty. Enough time to make a detour via the main boulevards: not far from the Opéra, where I have to retrieve my pen from a repair shop. Atypically, I decide to take the right-hand sidewalk on rue de la Chaussée-d'Antin. One of the first people I spot heading toward me is Nadja, looking as she did the first day. She walks as if trying not to see me. Like the first day, I retrace my steps to accompany her. She proves fairly incapable of explaining her presence in that street, where, to forestall further questions, she says she's looking for Dutch candies. Without realizing it, we have already made an about-face, and we go into the first café we come across. Nadja observes

*Doesn't this approach the extreme limit of the Surrealist aspiration, its *furthest ideal*?

The Nouvelle France (p. 52)

a certain distance toward me, even appears suspicious. She turns over my hat, no doubt to read my initials on the sweatband, though she claims she's doing it mechanically, out of a habit of trying to discover the nationality of certain men without them knowing. She admits that she'd intended to miss our rendezvous. I noticed when running into her that she was carrying the copy of *The Lost Steps* I'd lent her. It is now on the table and, from the top edge, I see that only several pages have been cut open. They're the ones containing a brief essay called "The New Spirit," which in fact relates a remarkable encounter that Louis Aragon, André Derain, and I each had one day, only several minutes apart. The indecisiveness we had all shown on that occasion; the difficulty we had a few moments later trying to characterize what had just happened to us; the strange, mystical call that drove Aragon and me to return to the places where that veritable sphinx had appeared in the guise of a charming woman—that sphinx who crossed from sidewalk to sidewalk, questioning the passersby, and who had sequentially ignored the three of us—and, in search of her, to *run* down all the streets that even tangentially connected those places; the hopelessness of that pursuit, given how much time had elapsed: that was what Nadja had immediately gravitated toward. She is surprised and disappointed that the narrative of that day's events did not seem to elicit any further comment from me. She presses me to explain the exact meaning I attribute to my report and, since I published it, how objective I feel it is. I'm forced to answer that I have no idea, that in such matters the only right I can claim is to record, that I was the primary victim of that deception, if deception there was, but I can see that she's not letting me off the hook. I read impatience in her eyes, then consternation. Perhaps she thinks I'm lying: there persists a certain awkwardness between us. When she mentions returning home, I offer to accompany her. She gives the driver the address of the Théâtre des Arts, which, she tells me, is a few doors down from her building. On the way, she stares at me at length, in silence. Then her eyelids close and reopen very quickly, as when you find yourself in the presence of someone you haven't seen in a long time, or that you never expected to see again, as if to signify that you "don't believe your eyes." A certain struggle appears to be raging in her, but suddenly she lets herself go, shuts her eyes completely, offers her lips . . .

Now she tells me of my power over her, the ability I have to make her think and do whatever I wish, perhaps more than I think I wish. Given this, she begs me not to undertake anything against her. She feels that nothing about her has been a secret to me, from well before we first met. A short scene in dialogue toward the end of "Soluble Fish," which seems to be all she has read of the *Manifesto* (a scene to which, moreover, I've never been able to ascribe a precise meaning and in which the characters remain opaque for me, their restlessness immune to interpretation, as if they had been brought there and carried off again by waves of sand), leaves her with the sense that she'd actually participated in it and even that she'd played the part—obscure, to say the least—of Hélène.* The location, the atmosphere, the actors' stances were exactly what I had imagined. She'd like to show me

*I've never personally known any woman by that name, which has always irritated me, just as I've always been enchanted by the name Solange. And yet, Mme Sacco, fortune teller, 3 rue des Usines, who has never been mistaken on my account, assured me at the beginning of that year that my thoughts were largely preoccupied by a "Hélène." Is this why, sometime after that, I became so interested in anything concerning the medium *Hélène Smith*? The conclusions I could draw from this would be similar to the ones dictated earlier by the fusion of two very disparate images in a dream. "Hélène is me," said Nadja.

Mme Sacco, fortune teller, 3 rue des Usines (p. 55)

"where it took place." I propose we have dinner together. A certain confusion must have entered her mind, as she has us driven, not to Île Saint-Louis, as she thinks, but to Place Dauphine, which curiously enough is the setting for another episode of "Soluble Fish," the one beginning "A kiss is so soon forgotten." (Place Dauphine is surely one of the most profoundly remote places I know, one of the worst wastelands in Paris. Whenever I've found myself there, I've felt the urge to leave gradually dissipate, and I've had to fight with myself to get free of a grip that was very soft, pleasantly insistent, and, ultimately, destructive. Moreover, I lived for a while in a hotel near that square, the City Hôtel, in which the comings and goings at all hours, for anyone who isn't satisfied with simple answers, were highly suspect.)

Daylight is fading. In order to be alone, we have the wine merchant serve us at an outdoor table. During the meal, for the first time, Nadja acts rather frivolously. A drunkard keeps hovering around us. He spews out loud, incoherent words, in an angry voice. Among those words, he keeps repeating one or two obscenities, which he emphasizes. His wife, watching from under the trees, merely calls out now and again, "Are you coming or what?" I try several times to shoo him away, but in vain. When our dessert arrives, Nadja begins looking around her. She is certain that an underground tunnel runs beneath our feet, starting at the Palais de Justice (she shows me from where in the Palais, slightly to the right of the white flight of steps) and snaking around the Hôtel Henri IV. She is disturbed by the idea of what has already happened in this square and what is yet to happen. While at this moment only two or three couples are fading into the twilight, she seems to see a crowd. "And the dead, the dead!" The drunkard continues to make lugubrious jokes. Nadja's

We have the wine merchant serve us at an outdoor table (p. 57)

eyes now roam over the apartment houses. "Over there, do you see that window? It's black, like all the others. Watch closely. In a minute, it will light up. It will be red." The minute passes. The window lights up. There are, in fact, red curtains. (I'm sorry, but I can't help it if this stretches the limits of credibility. Still, on a matter such as this, I'd be hard pressed to take sides: I'll simply *acknowledge* that the window was black, then became red, and that's all.) I confess that at this point, I start to get frightened, and so does Nadja. "How dreadful! Do you see what's happening in those trees? The blue and the wind, the blue wind. Only one other time did I see that blue wind run through those same trees. It was over there, from a window in the Henri IV,* and my friend, the second one I told you about, was getting ready to leave. And there was a voice saying: 'You're going to die, you're going to die.' I didn't want to die, but I felt so dizzy... I would surely have fallen if he hadn't pulled me back."

I think it's high time for us to go. All along the quays, I can feel her trembling. She's the one who wanted to walk back past the Conciergerie. She is very unrestrained, very trusting of me. Still, she's looking for something, she absolutely insists that we enter a courtyard, the nondescript courtyard of a police station that she quickly scans. "It's not here... But, tell me, why do you have to go to jail? What did you do? I was in jail once. Who was I? It was centuries ago. And you, back then, who were you?" We're again walking alongside the fence when suddenly Nadja refuses to take another step. There is, to the right, a window below street level that looks out on the moat; she cannot tear her eyes

*The hotel is directly opposite the building I was just speaking of, again for those who like simple solutions.

away from it. It's in front of that window, which looks disused, that we absolutely have to wait: this she knows. It's from there that everything could come. It's there that everything begins. She grips the fence with both hands so that I can't drag her away. She barely answers my questions. Tired of fighting, I end up waiting for her to resume our walk of her own free will. She is still thinking about the underground tunnel and probably believes we're at one of its exits. She wonders who she might have been in Marie Antoinette's entourage. Passing footsteps give her the tremors. I start to get worried, and loosening her hands one at a time, I finally oblige her to come away with me. More than half an hour has been spent like this. After crossing the bridge, we head toward the Louvre. Nadja seems constantly distracted. To bring her attention back to me, I recite for her a poem by Baudelaire, but the inflections of my voice inspire a new fright in her, aggravated by the memory of our kiss earlier: "a kiss that carried a threat." She halts once more, leans her elbows on the stone parapet from where her gaze, and mine, plunge into the river, which at that hour is sparkling with lights: "That hand, that hand on the Seine, why is there a flaming hand on the water? It's true that fire and water are the same thing. But what does that hand mean? How do you interpret it? Just let me watch that hand. Why do you want us to leave? What are you afraid of? You think I'm very sick, don't you? I'm not sick. But what does that mean for you, fire and water, a hand of fire on the water?" (Playfully:) "Not fortune, of course: fire and water are the same thing; fire and gold are completely different."

At around midnight, we arrive at the Tuileries, where she wants to sit for a moment. We are in front of a fountain, and she seems to be following the curve of its jet. "Those are your

She seems to be following the curve of its jet (p. 60)

thoughts and mine. See where they all start from, how high they rise, and how it's even prettier when they fall back down. And then they are immediately absorbed, taken up with the same force, again there's that broken surge, the fall... and so on indefinitely." I cry out: "But, Nadja, how strange! Where did you get that image, which is expressed in almost exactly the same way in a book you couldn't know and that I've just read?" (And I have to explain to her that it's the subject of a vignette, at the head of the third of Berkeley's *Three Dialogues Between Hylas and Philonous*, in the French edition of 1750, where it is accompanied by the caption: "Urget aquas vis sursum eadem, flectit que deorsum," which at the end of the book takes on particular significance vis-à-vis the defense of idealist philosophy.) But she isn't listening, her attention now absorbed by the doings of a man who has passed by us several times and whom she thinks she knows, as it isn't the first time she's been in these gardens at this time of night. That man, if it is indeed he, offered to marry her. It made her think about her little daughter, a child whose existence she reveals to me very cautiously, and whom she adores, especially because she is so unlike the other children, "with her idea of always plucking out dolls' eyes to see *what's behind* them." She knows that children are always drawn to her: wherever she is, they tend to flock around her, come smile at her. She is now speaking as if for herself alone, the things she says are of variable interest, her face is turned away from me, I'm starting to get tired. But, without any sign of impatience on my part: "Just one thing. I suddenly had the feeling I was going to cause you pain." (Turning toward me:) "It's over." We leave the gardens and soon stop once more, in a bar on rue Saint-Honoré called the Dauphin. She remarks that we've come from Place Dauphine

Urget aquas vis sursum eadem, flectit que deorsum.

TROISIÉME

DIALOGUE

HILONOUS. Hé bien, *Hyla*
quels ſont les fruits de vos m
ditations d'hier ? vous ont-e

At the head of the third of Berkeley's
Three Dialogues Between Hylas and Philonous . . . (p. 62)

to the Dauphin. (In the game that consists of looking for correspondences between a person and a given animal, people often agree that I'm a dolphin.) Nadja cannot bear the sight of a mosaic pattern that runs across the floor from the counter, and we have to leave the bar soon after we've entered. She gets out in front of the Théâtre des Arts. We agree to meet again at the Nouvelle France, but not until the day after tomorrow.

October 7.—I suffered a violent headache that, perhaps wrongly, I attribute to the emotions of the night before, as well as to the sustained effort of attention and accommodation I had to make. All morning long, too, I missed Nadja, chiding myself for not arranging to see her today. I'm dissatisfied with myself. I feel like I watch her too closely, but how can I do otherwise? How does she view me, judge me? It's unforgivable of me to keep seeing her if I don't love her. Don't I love her? When I'm near her, I'm nearer to the things that are near her. In the state she's in, she will surely need my help, one way or another, and without warning. Whatever she asks, it would be despicable of me to refuse: she's so pure, so free of earthly bonds, with such a fragile—but marvelous—hold on life. She was trembling yesterday, perhaps from cold. So lightly dressed. It would also be unforgivable if I didn't reassure her about the nature of my interest, if I didn't persuade her that she could never be just an object of curiosity for me, a mere whim, as she might believe. What is to be done? Resign myself to waiting until tomorrow afternoon—that's just impossible. What to do in the meantime, if I don't see her? And what if I never saw her again? I would no longer *know*. I would therefore deserve not to know. And I would never find it again. False annunciations exist, fleeting moments of grace, veritable death traps for the soul, the abyss, the abyss into which the splendidly mournful bird of divination has plummeted. What can I do, other than go at six o'clock to the bar where we had met previously? No chance of finding her there, of course, unless... But isn't "unless" where Nadja's great potential for intervention resides, well beyond luck?

I go out at three o'clock with my wife and a friend; in the taxi, we continue talking about Nadja, as we had done over lunch. Suddenly, as I'm paying no particular attention to the passersby, I don't know what rapid blur, there, on the left-hand sidewalk, at the entrance to rue Saint-Georges, makes me almost automatically rap on the window. It's as if Nadja had just walked by. I run haphazardly, in one of the three directions she might have taken. It is indeed she, now stopped, talking with a man who, it seemed to me, was with her earlier. She leaves him fairly quickly to join me. At the café, our conversation gets off to a difficult start. It's now been two days in a row that I've run into her: it's clear she is at my mercy. That said, she appears very reticent. Her financial situation is completely desperate, but to be able to improve it, she'd have to not know me. She makes me touch her dress, to show me how sturdy it is, "but at the expense of any other quality." She can't pile up any more debt, and she's dealing with threats from the manager of her hotel and his horrifying insinuations. She makes no secret of the means she would employ to earn money were it not for me, even though she no longer has the wherewithal to get her hair done so she could go to the Claridge, where, inevitably... "What can you do," she says with a laugh. "Money slips through my fingers. Anyway, now it's all gone. I did once find myself with twenty-five thousand francs, which my friend had left me. I was assured it would be very easy to *triple* that sum in a few days if I just went to The Hague to buy cocaine with it. They gave me thirty-five thousand more francs for the same purpose. Everything went off without a hitch. Two days later, I brought back nearly two kilos of drugs in my bag. The trip couldn't have been more pleasant. And yet, getting off the train, I heard a kind of voice telling me: 'You won't get through.' I was barely on the platform when a man I'd never seen before came up to me. 'Excuse me,' he said, 'am I indeed speaking to Miss D. . . .?'—'Yes, but, forgive me, I don't know . . .'—'No matter, miss, here's my card,' and he brought me to the police station. There, they asked me what was in my handbag. Naturally, I told them what it was and opened it to show them. They let me go the same day, thanks to the intervention of a friend, a lawyer or judge named G. They didn't ask me anything else, and as for me, I was so shaken that I forgot to mention that not all of it was in my bag; they should also look under my hatband. But what they would have found there wouldn't have been worth the trouble. I kept it for myself. I swear that's been over for a long time." She's now unfolding a letter that she hands me. It's from a man she met one Sunday coming out of the Théâtre-Français. He must be an office employee, since he waited several days to write to her *and not before the beginning of the month*. She could telephone him now, him or someone else, but she can't make up her mind to do it. No question that money slips through her fingers. I ask how much she needs right away: five hundred francs. Not having it on me, I offer to give it to her the next day. All her worry seems to evaporate. I savor once again her adorable mix of lightness and fervor. Respectfully I kiss her very pretty teeth. She, slowly, solemnly, the second time several notes higher than the first: "The communion takes place in silence . . . The communion takes place in silence." It is, she explains, that this kiss leaves her with the impression of something sacred, in which her teeth "served as the host."

October 8.—On awakening, I open a letter from Aragon in Italy, containing the reproduction of the center detail of a painting by Uccello that I didn't know. The painting's title is *The Profanation of the Host.** Toward the end of the day, which has passed without further incident, I go to our usual bar (the Nouvelle France), where I wait for Nadja in vain. More than ever, I dread her disappearance. My only resort is to try to find where she lives, somewhere around the Théâtre des Arts. It doesn't take long: the third hotel I try, the Hôtel du Théâtre on rue de Chéroy. Not finding her in, I leave a note asking how to get her what she needed so urgently the day before yesterday.

October 9.—Nadja called while I was out. To the person who answered the phone, and who asked on my behalf where she could be reached, she answered: "No one can reach me." But a little later, she sent a pneumatique inviting me to come to the bar at five-thirty. I indeed find her there. Her absence the day before was the result of a misunderstanding: we had, that one time, arranged to meet at the Régence, and it was

*I saw it reproduced in its entirety only several months later. It struck me as being laden with hidden meanings and, all things considered, very difficult to interpret.

The Profanation of the Host (p. 67)

I who had forgotten. I give her the money.* She bursts into tears. We are alone when an old peddler comes in, a kind I've never seen before. He offers us several crudely colored pages from a history of France. The one he holds out to me, which he insists I take, depicts notable episodes from the reigns of Louis VI and Louis VII (and in fact, I have just been heavily immersed in that period, as it's the time of the Court of Love, and had been imagining very intensely how life was conceived of back then). The old man makes a number of jumbled comments about each of the illustrations; I can't follow what he's saying about Suger. For the two francs I give him, then two more to make him go away, he is absolutely insistent on leaving us all his pictures, as well as a dozen glossy color postcards of women. Impossible to dissuade him. He backs away: "God bless you, miss. God bless you, sir." Now Nadja has me read letters that she recently received. These letters are of little interest to me. Some are tearful, others declamatory, still others ridiculous, all signed by this G. she'd mentioned previously. G....—but isn't that the name of the criminal court judge who, the other day at the murder trial of Mrs. Sierri, accused of poisoning her lover, let loose with the odious remark that the defendant had "bitten the hand that fed her" (*laughter in the court*)? And in fact, Paul Éluard had asked us to find that name for him, which he couldn't remember and had left blank in the manuscript of his "Review of the Press" for the next issue of *La Révolution surréaliste*. I notice with some queasiness that printed on the backs of the envelopes I'm looking at is a pair of scales.

*Three times the agreed amount, which, as I've just realized, is not devoid of coincidence.

Pl. [illegible]

HISTOIRE DE LA FRANCE

Les Croisades. — Concile de Clermont (1095) — Pierre l'Ermite prêchant la 1re Croisade — Assemblée de Vézelay (1146) — Saint Bernard prêchant la 2e Croisade

La plus brillante expédition féodale, la 1re Croisade, fut entreprise pour délivrer la Palestine de la domination des Musulmans. A la voix de Pierre l'Ermite au concile de Clermont, que le pape Urbain II présidait en personne, le peuple et les barons prirent la croix au cri de « Dieu le veut! » La pauvre armée composée d'hommes, de femmes et d'enfants conduite par **Pierre l'Ermite** et **Gauthier-sans-Avoir** fut écrasée par les Turcs.

Les Croisés, disciplinés et dirigés par **Godefroy de Bouillon**, débarquèrent en Asie; ils furent vainqueurs à Dorylée, s'emparèrent d'Antioche et entrèrent dans Jérusalem, après un assaut furieux le 15 juillet 1099.

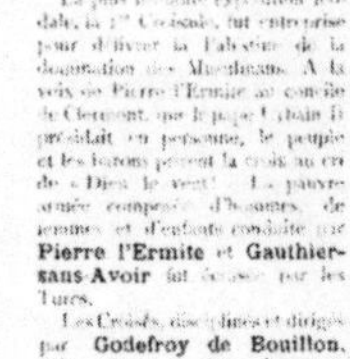

Louis VI le Gros (1108) essaya de chasser de Normandie **Henri Ier** roi d'Angleterre et sut intimider l'empereur d'Allemagne **Henri V** qui voulait envahir la France.

Au plus fort d'un combat, un soldat anglais saisit par la bride le cheval du roi de France en criant : « Le roi est pris ! » — « On ne prend jamais le roi, pas même aux échecs » riposta le roi Louis VI, et il tua l'Anglais.

Louis VII et Suger, Abbé de St-Denis

Louis VII (1137) prêché par **St Bernard** et voulant expier le massacre de Vitry prit la Croix. Cette 2e Croisade fut désastreuse : le roi ne put s'emparer de Damas et revint après avoir perdu toute son armée.

Louis VII, dit le Jeune, était faible, indécis ; il eut pour conseiller **Suger**, abbé de St-Denis, qui le dirigea pendant les dix premières années de son règne et prit la régence au moment de la seconde Croisade.

Pendant deux ans, Suger empêcha le divorce du roi qui devait enlever l'Aquitaine aux Capétiens et qui fut consommé quelques mois après sa mort, au concile de Beaugency.

Les règnes de Louis VI et de Louis VII virent les premiers progrès de la bourgeoisie qui s'organisa en communes et en villes franches.

Maison de propagande [illegible] rue [illegible], Paris — [illegible] Imp. [illegible]

In fact, I have just been heavily immersed in that period . . . (p. 69)

October 10.—We have dinner on Quai Malaquais, at the restaurant Delaborde. The waiter is exceedingly clumsy. It's as if he's mesmerized by Nadja. He fusses at our table for no reason, scraping imaginary crumbs from the tablecloth, moving her handbag around, proving utterly incapable of remembering our order. Nadja laughs up her sleeve and warns me that it's not over yet. And indeed, while he serves the other tables normally, he splashes wine outside of our glasses and, while taking infinite care to set a dish in front of one of us, he jostles the other and sends it crashing to the floor. Over the course of the meal (and this, too, is almost incredible), I count eleven broken plates. It's true that whenever he enters the dining room, he is facing us; then he raises his eyes to Nadja and seems to have a dizzy spell. It's at once comical and painful. He ends up not daring to approach our table, making it extremely difficult for us to finish our dinner. Nadja is not at all surprised. She knows she has this power over certain men, for instance over blacks, who, wherever she might be, are compelled to come talk to her. She tells me that at three o'clock, at the ticket window of Le Peletier metro station, someone handed her a new two-franc coin, which she kept tightly gripped in her hand all the way down the stairs. To the ticket-taker at the turnstile, she asked: "Heads or tails?" He answered tails. He won. "You were asking, miss, if you would see your friend later on. You will see him."

We walk along the quays toward the Institut de France. She speaks again of the man she calls Special Friend, to whom she says she owes being who she is. "If not for him, I'd just be the lowest of streetwalkers." I learn that he used to put her under hypnosis every evening, after dinner. It took her several months to realize it. He made her recount how she'd spent her day, in every detail, praising what he considered good and criticizing the rest. And after that, a physical discomfort in her head would always prevent her from doing those things he must have forbidden. That man, lost in his white beard, who wanted her to know nothing about him, is like a king to her. Wherever she went with him, it seemed as if people respectfully stood at attention as he passed by. And yet, sometime later, she saw him one evening, on a bench in a metro station, looking very weary, very disheveled, and very aged.

We have arrived at the start of rue de Seine, which we turn onto, as Nadja does not want to keep walking straight ahead. She is again distracted, tells me she's following a streak of lightning that a hand is slowly tracing across the sky. "Always that hand." She shows it to me in reality, on a poster, a short way past the Dorbon bookstore. There is indeed, high above us, a red hand with a pointing index finger, advertising who knows what. She absolutely must touch that hand, which she jumps up several times to reach and against which she finally manages to slap hers. "The hand of fire, that's about you, you know, it's you." She remains silent for a while, and I think she has tears in her eyes. Then suddenly, placing herself in front of me, practically blocking my path, with that extraordinary way she has of calling me, as you might call out to someone from room to room in an empty castle: "André? André?... You'll write a novel about me. I promise. Don't say no. Beware: everything fades, everything disappears. Something of us must remain... But it doesn't matter: you'll pick another name, and that name, believe me when I tell you, is very important. It has to be a little like the name of fire, since fire always enters into it where you're concerned. The hand, too, but that's less critical than fire. What I see is a flame starting from the wrist, like this"—with a gesture of palming a card—"which makes the hand burn up immediately, vanish in the blink of an eye. You'll find a Latin or Arabic pseudonym.* Promise me. You have to." She uses a new image to help me picture how she lives: it's like in the morning when she takes her bath and her body floats away as she stares at the surface of the water. "I am the thought on the bath in a room without mirrors."

She'd forgotten to tell me about the strange incident that happened to her yesterday evening, at around eight o'clock, when, believing she was alone, she was singing and dancing as she walked under the arcades of the Palais Royal. An old woman emerged from a closed doorway, and she thought the woman was going to ask for a handout. But all she wanted was a pencil. Nadja lent her hers and the woman made a show of scribbling some words on a calling card before slipping it under the door. She took the opportunity to hand Nadja a similar card, explaining that she had come to see "Madam Camée" and that the latter was unfortunately not in. The scene took place in front of a shop, on whose facade one could read the words for stone cameos: CAMÉES DURS. The woman looked a lot like a witch. I study the diminutive card that Nadja insists on giving me: "Madam Aubry-Abrivard, woman of letters, 20 rue de Varenne, 4th floor, right." This episode demands some clarification. Nadja, who has thrown a flap of her cape over her shoulder, suddenly and with remarkable ease looks like the Devil as he appears in Romantic etchings. It is very dark and very cold. Moving closer to her, I'm appalled to see that she's trembling, literally, "like a leaf."

*Apparently the doors of many Arab houses bear the inscription of a red hand, rendered more or less schematically, which is the "hand of Fatima."

CAMÉES DURS (p. 73)

October 11.—Paul Éluard went to the address on that card. He found no one home. Pinned to the door, upside down, was an envelope bearing the words: "Today, October 11th, Mme Aubry-Abrivard will return very late, but will return most certainly." I'm in a bad mood following a conversation I had that afternoon, which went on too long for no good reason. On top of which, Nadja arrived late, and I'm expecting nothing sensational from her. We wander through the streets, side by side but very apart. She repeats at various moments a sentence whose syllables she articulates more and more distinctly: "Time is a tease. Time is a tease because everything has to come in its time." It's irritating to watch her read the menus outside restaurants and pun on the names of the dishes. I'm bored. We walk along boulevard Magenta past the Sphinx Hôtel. She points out the neon sign bearing those words, which made her decide to register there her first night in Paris. She stayed for several months, her only visitor being Special Friend, who passed for her uncle.

October 12.—I asked Max Ernst if he would agree to do Nadja's portrait. But Madam Sacco predicted that he would meet a woman named Nadia or Natasha whom he wouldn't like and who would cause physical harm to the woman he loves. This contraindication is enough for us. A little after four o'clock, in a café on boulevard des Batignolles, I again have to pretend to read letters from G., full of entreaties and accompanied by idiotic poems, like a poor man's Musset. Then Nadja shows me a drawing, the first I've seen by her, that she made the other day at the Régence while waiting for me. She's eager to explain what the major components of the drawing mean, except for the rectangular mask, about

Boulevard Magenta past the Sphinx Hôtel (p. 75)

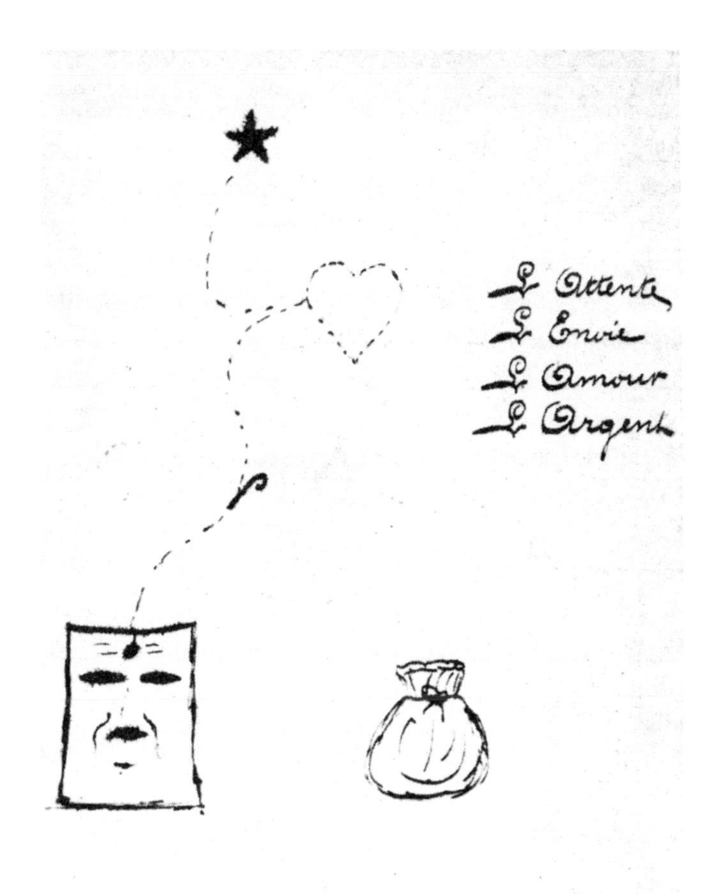

Except for the rectangular mask, about which she can say nothing… (p. 75)

which she can say nothing, other than that's how it appeared to her. The black spot in the middle of the forehead is the nail on which it is pinned up; following the dotted line, we first come to a hook; the black star, toward the top, represents the Idea. But what, according to Nadja, constitutes the primary interest of the sheet, without my being able to understand why, is the calligraphic shape of the *L*'s. After dinner, near the garden of the Palais Royal, her dream seems to take a mythological turn that I had never before seen in her. For a moment, she artfully assumes the elusive character of Melusine, creating a very striking illusion of her. Then she asks me point blank: "Who killed the Gorgon, tell me, who?" I have more and more trouble following her soliloquy, which her long silences begin to render unintelligible. It's already late when I suggest we get out of Paris. And so we head to the Gare Saint-Lazare, where I buy tickets for Saint-Germain. Our train leaves before our eyes. We have to wait almost an hour for the next one, at eleven-thirty. We pace around the station concourse. Immediately, like the other day, a drunkard starts prowling near us. He complains that he can't find his way, wants me to guide him to the exit. Nadja is no longer acting distant. She points out to me that everyone, even if in a hurry, is turning to look at us, which is true; that it's not just her they're looking at, but *us*. "They can't believe it, you see. They can't get over seeing us together. It's so rare, the fire that's in your eyes, and in mine."

We're now alone in a first-class compartment. All her confidence, all her attention, all her hopes are again focused on me. What if we got off at Le Vésinet? She'd like to walk in the forest awhile. Why not? But suddenly, as I'm kissing her, she cries out. "There" (pointing to the top of the outside window). "There's someone out there. I clearly saw an upside-down head just now." I reassure her as best I can. Five minutes later, the same thing: "I'm telling you, he's there, wearing a cap. No, it's not a vision. I know when it's a vision." I lean out the window: no one on the running board, nor on the stepladder of the next car. And yet Nadja swears she wasn't mistaken. She stares obstinately at the top of the window and remains very agitated. Just to make sure, I lean out once more. I barely have time to glimpse, very distinctly, the disappearing head of a man flat on his stomach on the roof of the car, right above our compartment, who is in fact wearing a uniform cap. No doubt a railway employee, who could easily get there from the upper deck of the second-class car next to ours. At the next station, as Nadja stands near the door and I watch from the window, a lone man, before leaving the station, blows her a kiss. A second man does the same, then a third. She receives these kinds of homages with complacency and gratitude. They never fail to happen, and she seems quite attached to them. At Le Vésinet, with everything closed, impossible to find lodgings for the night. Roaming the forest no longer seems very enticing. We decide to wait for the next train to Saint-Germain. At around one in the morning, we wind up at the Hôtel Prince de Galles. Walking past the château, Nadja wanted to be Madame de Chevreuse; so gracefully did she hide her face behind the heavy, nonexistent plume of her hat!

Can it be that this frantic pursuit ends here? Pursuit of what, I don't know, but *pursuit,* to call upon all the artifices of intellectual seduction. Nothing—not the glitter of rare metals like sodium when they're cut—nor the phosphorescence of quarries in certain regions—nor the brilliance of the admirable glow that rises from pits—nor the crackling of the wood of a clock that I throw on the fire so that it might die while chiming the hour—nor the attraction exerted, despite everything, by *The Embarkation for Cythera* when you realize that it stages multiple poses of a single couple—nor the majesty of landscapes surrounding reservoirs—nor the charm of sections of wall from buildings under demolition, with their fleurettes and shadows of chimneys: none of that, none of what constitutes my own personal light, has been forgotten. Who were we in the face of reality, the reality that I now know was lying at Nadja's feet like a cunning dog? What latitude could we possibly have been on, prone to our symbolic frenzy, sometimes prey to the demon of analogy, seeing ourselves as the object of extreme actions and singular, special attentions? How could it be that, finally launched together so far from earth, in the brief pauses our marvelous stupor allowed us, we managed to exchange a few remarkably concordant views, above the smoking rubble of outmoded thinking and sempiternal life? From the first day to the last, I considered Nadja a free genius, like one of those ethereal spirits that certain magic practices allow you to engage with momentarily but that you could never subdue. As for her, I know that in the strongest sense of the word she sometimes saw me as a god, believed I was the sun. I remember, too—and at this moment, nothing could be more beautiful or more tragic—I remember appearing to her black and cold, like a stricken man prostrate at the feet of the Sphinx. I've seen her fern-colored eyes *open* in the morning onto a world in which the beating wings of great hope are scarcely discernible from other sounds, the sounds of terror; a world onto which until then I had only seen eyes close. I know that for Nadja, this *departure*, starting from a point that it would be extremely rare and foolhardy to even try to attain, happened in defiance of everything usually invoked when one drowns, deliberately far from the life raft, at the cost of everything that constitutes the false but practically irresistible compensations of life. At the very top of that castle over there, in the right-hand tower, is a room that probably no one would take us to visit, that we would be foolish to visit—no reason to try—but that, according to Nadja, is all we'd need to know of Saint-Germain, for example.* I feel great affinity for men who let themselves be shut up in a museum at night so they can contemplate, illicitly and at their leisure, a woman's portrait by the light of a covered lantern. From then on, they surely know much more about that woman than we do. It's possible that life demands to be decoded like a cryptogram. Secret stairways; frames from which the canvas suddenly slides out and disappears, to be replaced by an archangel brandishing a sword or by those who must always push forward; buttons that you press indirectly to trigger the vertical or horizontal displacement of an entire room and a lightning change of scenery: we can conceive of the greatest mental adventure as a voyage of this type to the paradise of pitfalls. Who is the true Nadja: the one who told me she once wandered with an archaeologist for an entire night through the forest of Fontainebleau, hunting for vestiges of stone that, presumably, they could easily have looked for during the day—but since it was the man's passion!—in other words, the always inspired and

*It was Louis VI who, at the beginning of the twelfth century, built a royal castle in the forest of Laye, the origin of the present château and of the town of Saint-Germain.

At the very top of that castle over there, in the right-hand tower . . . (p. 81)

inspiring creature who preferred the street (which for her was the only site of valid experience), open to questions from any human being set out on a wild dream; or (why not admit it?) the one who *fell* sometimes, because others felt entitled to speak to her, because they saw in her only the poorest and most vulnerable of women?

I sometimes reacted with terrible anger against the overly detailed stories she would tell me of her past life, from which I judged, no doubt rather superficially, that her dignity had not emerged intact. An incident she told me about for no apparent reason, on the afternoon of October 13, involving a punch in the face that made her spurt blood one day in the dining room of Brasserie Zimmer, a punch received from a man whom she allowed herself the wicked pleasure of refusing simply because he was coarse—she had called for help several times, and before running away made sure to bleed all over the man's clothes—almost managed to alienate me from her forever. I can't describe the feeling of absolute hopelessness that her smirking account of this horrible episode aroused in me, but after hearing it I wept for a long time, wept as I thought I could no longer weep. I wept at the idea that I *shouldn't* ever see Nadja again, not that I couldn't. Of course, I didn't blame her for not hiding from me what I now found so devastating—rather, I was grateful—but the thought of her having once been in such dire straits, and that there might be other such days for her on the horizon, was more than I could bear. She was so touching at that moment, doing nothing to break my resolve, but instead drawing from her tears the strength to urge me to follow through on it! Bidding me farewell, in Paris, she nonetheless couldn't keep from adding in a murmur that it was impossible, but then did nothing to try to make it more impossible. If it was forever, that was entirely up to me.

I saw Nadja many times after that. Her thoughts became clearer for me, their expression lighter, deeper, more original. At the same time, the irreparable disaster that implicated the most humanly defined part of her, the disaster of which I'd had an inkling that day, might gradually have drawn us apart. Enchanted as I still was by her way of living, ever miraculous and based on pure intuition, I was also increasingly alarmed by the sense that, when I left her side, she got caught up again in the turbulence around her, relentlessly forcing her to make concessions, such as having to eat, or sleep. For a while, I tried to provide her the wherewithal, since by now she could count only on me for help. But I highly doubt that I helped her to resolve her financial difficulties by more conventional means. Most days she appeared content just to have me be present, paying no attention to what I said, or to my boredom when she carried on about this or that or fell silent. It would be pointless for me to list here the many odd occurrences—which we witnessed together or apart—that could be of interest only to us, those events that ultimately incline me toward a kind of finalism that would explain the essential character of every event, the way that some have absurdly claimed to explain the essential character of all things.* As time goes by, I prefer to remember only a few phrases, ones she said to me or that she rapidly jotted down in my presence; phrases in which I hear most clearly her tone of voice and which still resonate strongly in me:

*It goes without saying that any notion of teleological justification in this regard is discarded in advance.

"With the end of my breath, which is the beginning of yours."

"If you wished it, I would be nothing for you, or just a trace."

"The lion's claw grips the breast of the vine."

"Pink is better than black, but the two go together."

"Before the mystery. Man of stone, understand me."

"You are my master. I am only an atom respiring at the corner of your lips, or expiring. I want to touch serenity with a finger wet with tears."

"Why that scale wavering in the darkness of a pit filled with lumps of coal?"

"Don't burden your thoughts with the weight of your shoes."

"I knew everything. I tried so hard to read into my rivers of tears."

Nadja invented a marvelous flower for me, *The Lovers' Flower*. It was over lunch in the country that this flower appeared to her, and I witnessed her inability to render it properly. She came back to it several times after, trying to improve on the drawing and give the two sets of eyes a different expression. It's under this sign in particular that we should place the time we spent together; it remains the graphic symbol that gave Nadja the key to all the others. Several times she attempted to draw my portrait with my hair standing on end, as if sucked upright in long flames by the wind. Those flames also formed the belly of an eagle whose heavy wings drooped on either side of my head. Following an inopportune comment that I made about one of her last drawings, the best of the lot, she unfortunately sliced off the entire bottom portion, by far the richest and strangest part. The drawing dated November 18, 1926, features a symbolic portrait of the two of us: a mermaid—which is how she always pictured herself, from behind and from that angle—holds in her hand a roll of paper; a monster with glaring eyes has the upper part of its body caught in a kind of eagle-headed vase, filled with feathers representing ideas. For me, the most obscure one remains *The Cat's Dream*, which depicts the animal trying to escape on its hind legs, not realizing that it's tethered to the ground by a weight and suspended from a rope that is also the outsized wick of an upside-down lamp. It was hastily cut out based on an apparition. Another cutout, this one in two parts so that the angle of the head could be varied, is the assemblage composed of a woman's face and a hand. *The Devil's Greeting*, like *The Cat's Dream*, illustrates an apparition. The drawing shaped like a helmet, and another one titled *A Nebulous Character*, too difficult to reproduce, are of a different type: they respond to her taste for seeking in the complex patterns of fabric, wood knots, or cracks in old walls outlines that aren't there but that you can easily come to see in them. In this drawing, we clearly make out the face of the Devil; a woman's head with a bird pecking at her lips; the hair, torso, and tail of a mermaid seen from behind; the head of an elephant; a sea lion; another woman's face; a snake and several other snakes; a heart; a kind of cow or buffalo head; branches of the tree of good and evil; and a few dozen other elements that the reproduction doesn't capture but that together form a real shield of Achilles. I should underscore the presence of two animal horns, near the upper-right margin, a presence that Nadja herself couldn't explain: they always appeared to her in that form, as if what they were related to was meant to obstinately mask the mermaid's face (this is especially evident in the drawing on the back of a postcard).

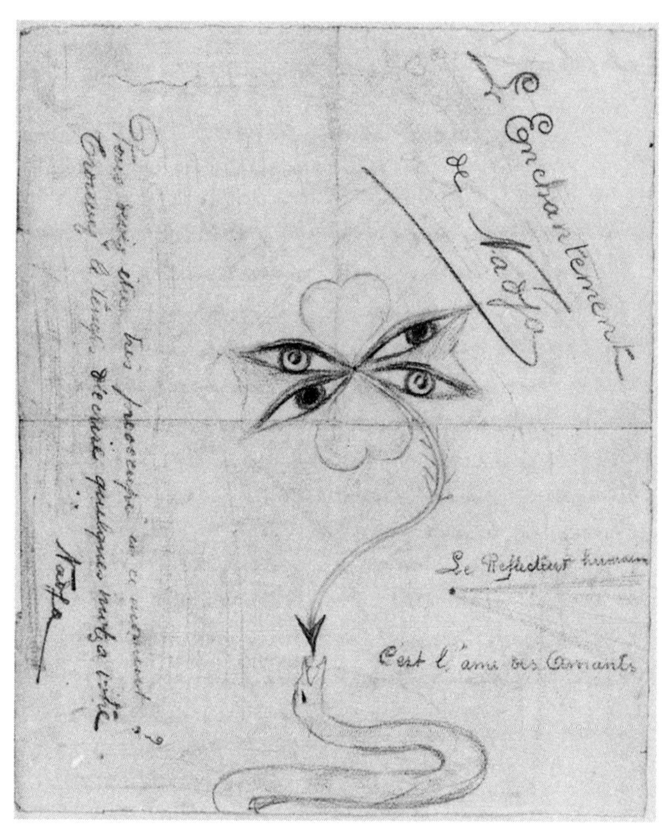

The Lovers' Flower (p. 85)

A symbolic portrait of the two of us (p. 86)

The Cat's Dream (p. 86)

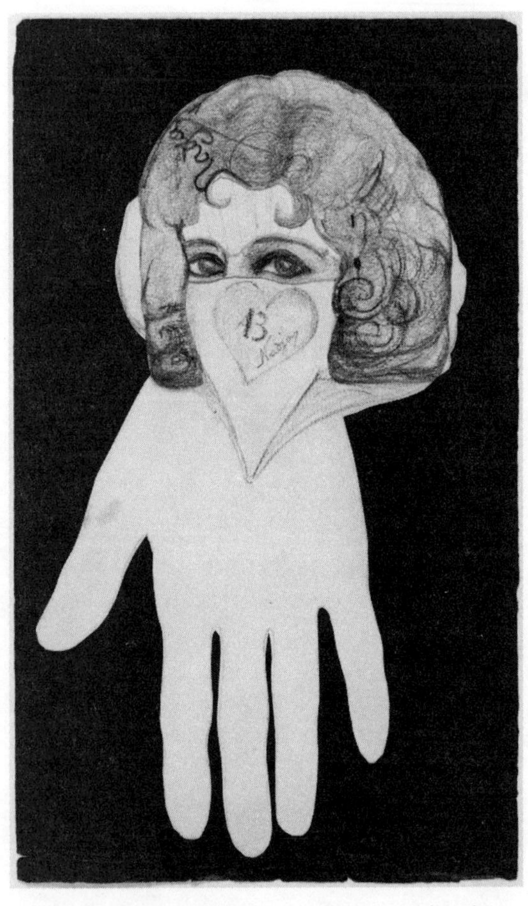

So that the angle of the head could be varied (p. 86)

Drawings by Nadja

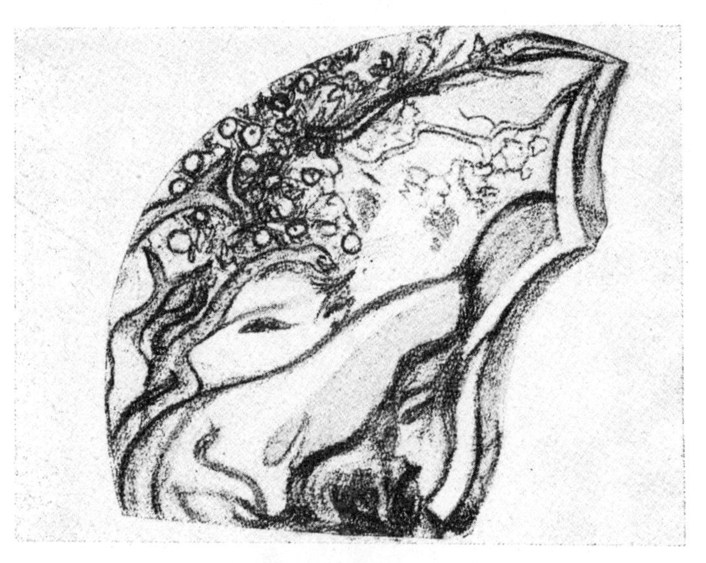

A real shield of Achilles (p. 86)

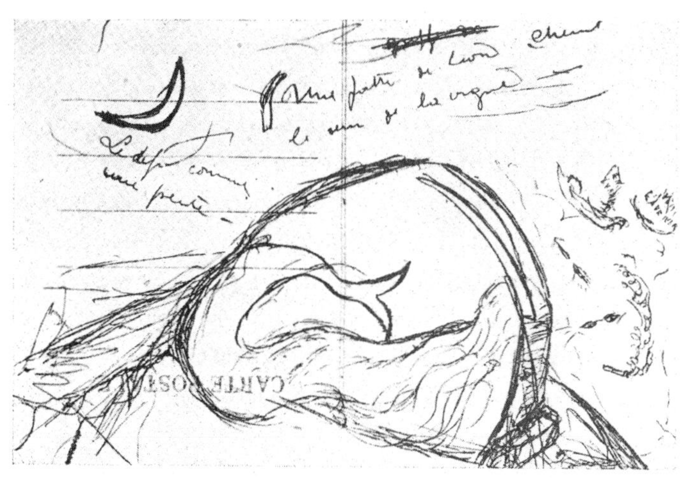

On the back of a postcard (p. 86)

Several days later, in fact, Nadja, visiting me at home, *recognized* those horns as the ones on a large Guinean mask that had once belonged to Henri Matisse, which I've always loved and feared because of its monumental crest, like a railway signal, but which she could not have seen as she did unless *inside the library*. On the same occasion, in a painting by Braque (*Man with a Guitar*), she recognized the nail and the rope, beside the figure, that have always intrigued me; and in the triangular painting by de Chirico (*The Anxious Journey* or *The Enigma of Fatality*—the titles of this painter's canvases are in dispute), the famous hand of fire. A conical mask from New Britain island, made of elderberry pith and reeds, made her cry out: "Goodness, Chimène!" A statuette of a seated cacique struck her as especially threatening. She lengthily commented on the particularly abstruse meaning of one of Max Ernst's paintings (*Men Shall Know Nothing of This*), in perfect alignment with the detailed notes on the back of the canvas. Another fetish object that I no longer possess was for her the god of slander; still another, from Easter Island (the first indigenous object I ever owned), said to her: "I love you! I love you!"

Nadja also depicted herself many times in the guise of Melusine, the mythical figure to whom she appeared to feel closest. I saw how she made every attempt to transform that semblance into reality, insisting that her hairdresser part her hair in five places at the forehead, so that it would look like a star. Two other tresses had to be coiled in front of her ears like ram's horns, winding horns being another of her frequent motifs. She liked to draw herself in the shape of a butterfly, its body formed by a Mazda (Nadja) light bulb, toward which rose a charmed serpent. (Since then, I'm troubled whenever I see the lit Mazda billboard on the main boulevards, which occupies almost the entire facade of the former Vaudeville theater, and on which two rams are in fact charging at each other, in a rainbow of light.) But the drawings Nadja showed me the last time I visited her, still unfinished, and which must have been lost in the tempest that carried her off, showed a whole new level of skill. (She had never drawn before we met.) On a table, before an open book, a cigarette posed on an ashtray from which serpentine smoke insidiously escapes; a globe of the world, split apart to hold lilies, in the hands of a very beautiful woman; all of it carefully arranged to allow for the descent of what she called *the human reflector*, held out of reach by talons. She considered this one "the best of all."

It had been some time since I'd stopped seeing eye to eye with Nadja. To tell the truth, maybe we had never seen eye to eye, at least when it came to dealing with basic matters of existence. She had chosen once and for all to take no notice of them, not to worry about punctuality, to make no distinction between her sometimes trifling remarks and the ones that meant so much to me, to disregard my momentary moods or my frequent difficulty in overlooking her blatant lapses of attention. As I've noted, she didn't mind telling me, in unsparing detail, about the most appalling misadventures of her life, or being inappropriately flirtatious while I waited, with furrowed brow, for her to finally move on to something else, for of course there was never any chance of her acting *naturally*. So many times, when at my wit's end, despairing of making her see her true worth, I almost fled from her—ready to meet up with her the next day, when she

The nail and the rope, beside the figure, that have always intrigued me (p. 94)

The Anxious Journey or *The Enigma of Fatality* (p. 94)

“Goodness, Chimène!” (p. 94)

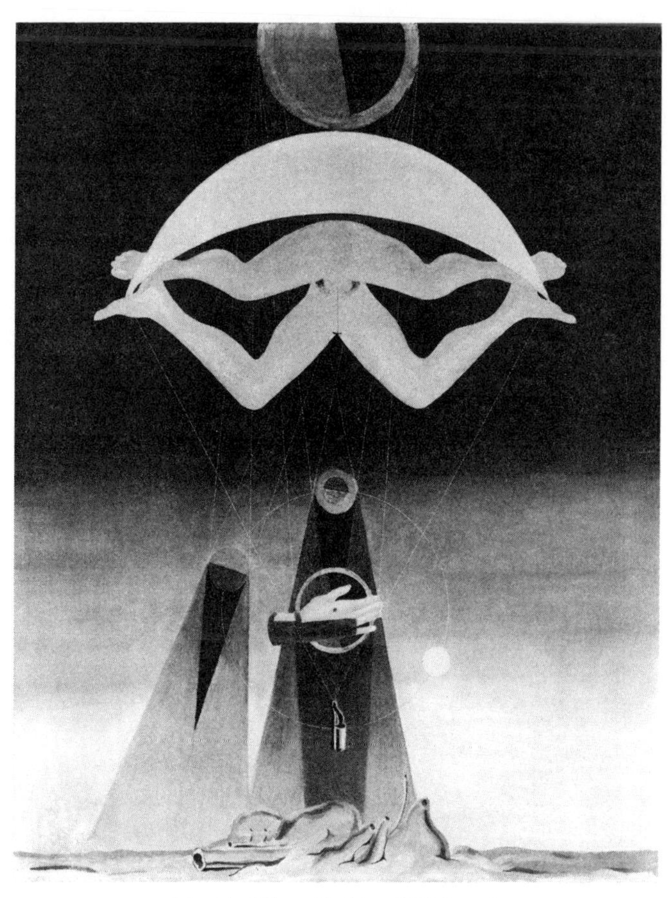

Men Shall Know Nothing of This (p. 94)

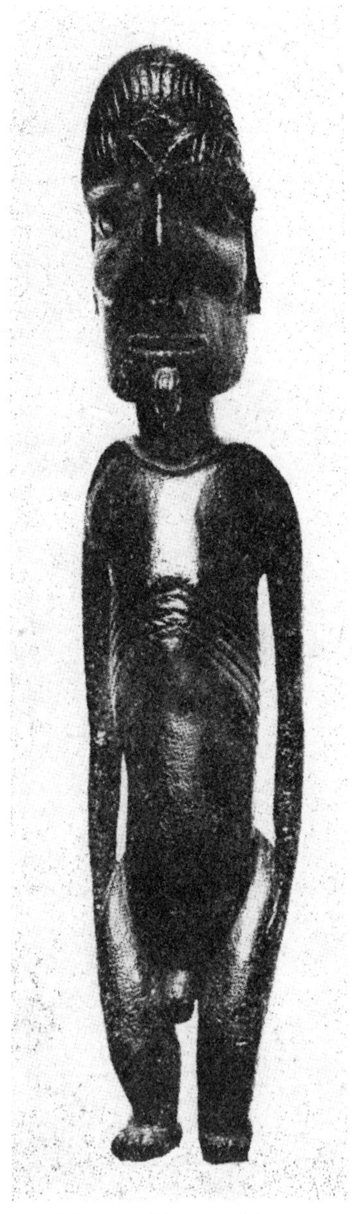

"I love you! I love you!" (p. 94)

The lit Mazda billboard on the main boulevards (p. 94)

The Soul of Wheat (drawing by Nadja)

was again the way she could be when not desperate, berating myself for my severity and begging her forgiveness! Deplorable as this was, it's also true that she treated me with less and less consideration, that we sometimes got into violent arguments, which she aggravated by ascribing them to mediocre causes that didn't exist. Whatever allows us to live another person's life without ever wishing for more than they're willing to give; to be amply satisfied with seeing them move or stand still, speak or be silent, wake or sleep, did not exist for me, had never existed: that was only too certain. It could hardly have been otherwise, given Nadja's world, in which everything so quickly took on an appearance of rise or fall. But this is a retrospective judgment, and it might be rash of me to say that it couldn't have been otherwise. Whatever desire or even illusion I might have had to the contrary, perhaps I was simply unequal to what she was offering me. But what was she offering me? It doesn't matter. Only love, in the sense that I understand it—that is, mysterious, improbable, unique, staggering, *certain* love; love that can overcome any obstacle—could have wrought a miracle in this case.

A few months ago, they came to tell me Nadja had gone mad. Following some eccentricities that she apparently engaged in in the corridors of her hotel, she had been committed to an insane asylum in the Vaucluse. Others can pontificate needlessly on this fact, which will surely strike them as the inevitable outcome of all that precedes. Those who are better informed will lose no time in combing through what I've reported about Nadja, parsing her already delirious ideas for their relative importance, and perhaps they will ascribe a terribly determinant value to my intervention in her life, an intervention that encouraged the development of those ideas. As for all those who think, "Ah! well, then," or "You see what I mean," or "I thought as much," or "Under those conditions," and other such low-rent morons, it goes without saying that I prefer to leave them be. The main thing is that, for Nadja, I don't imagine there's much difference between the inside of an asylum and the outside. Unfortunately, there must be some difference all the same, if only because of the grating of a key in a lock; the miserly view of the garden; the smugness of those who interrogate you when you least feel like it, falsely ingratiating themselves, like that Professor Claude at Sainte-Anne Hospital, with his dunce's forehead and obtuse expression ("People are out to get you, is that it?"—"No, sir."—"He's lying, last week he told me they were out to get him." Or else: "So, you hear voices. Well, are they voices like mine?"—"No, sir."—"Fine, he's suffering from auditory hallucinations," etc.); the uniform that is as abject as any uniform; and even the effort required to adapt to such surroundings—for these are, after all, surroundings and, as such, they demand that you adapt to some extent. If you have ever been in an asylum, you know that they *make* lunatics there, just as penal facilities make criminals. Is there anything more despicable than those so-called institutions of social preservation, where, for a peccadillo, a minor external breach of propriety or common sense, they throw an individual in with others whose presence can only be injurious, and where they systematically deprive him of contact with anyone who has a better developed moral or practical sense? The newspapers report that at the last international psychiatric conference, in the very first session, the delegates were unanimous in condemning the persistent popular notion that it's as hard to leave an asylum today as it once was a convent; that people who never had any business being

Like that Professor Claude at Sainte-Anne Hospital. (p. 104)

there, or no longer have any, are held in them for life; that public safety is not nearly as endangered as they want us to believe. And all the psychiatrists vehemently highlighted one or two cases to inflate their argument and clamored out catastrophic instances when this or that seriously ill patient was wrongly or prematurely released. Since their responsibility is always implicated in such instances, they made it clear that, when in doubt, they'd rather abstain. Yet, to my mind, this is not the real issue. The atmosphere inside insane asylums is such that it cannot fail to exert the most debilitating, pernicious influence upon those confined in them, along the exact same lines as the debilitation that first brought them there. This, further complicated by the fact that any demand, any protest, any hint of intolerance only ends up branding you as unsociable (for, paradoxical as it seems, they nonetheless require you to be sociable in those places); that it only serves to stack up another symptom against you; that not only can it impede your recovery, assuming such a thing is possible, but it can actually prevent your condition from remaining stable and instead make it worse. Hence the tragically rapid deterioration that we witness in asylums, which in most cases is probably not due to a single cause. When it comes to mental illness, we have every reason to denounce the almost inevitable degeneration from acute attack to chronic state. Given the peculiar and late-blooming development of psychiatry, we can, under such conditions, hardly talk about cures. I believe that the most conscientious psychiatrists don't even think in those terms. True, there are no longer arbitrary internments of the sort we used to hear about, since such detentions (of the most horrifying kind) are now triggered by an obvious and objectively certifiable action, abnormal in character and preferably committed in public. But as I see it, any internment is arbitrary. I persist in not understanding why someone would deprive a human being of his freedom. They locked up Sade, they locked up Nietzsche, they locked up Baudelaire. The procedure that consists in taking you unawares at night, binding you in a straitjacket or other means of subjugation, is no different from the police slipping a gun into your pocket. I know that if I were insane and had been locked up for several days, I'd take advantage of a *remission* in my delirium to murder in cold blood anyone, preferably the doctor, who came near me. At least then I'd be able, like the acutely agitated, to live in solitary confinement. Perhaps they'd leave me the hell alone.

The general contempt in which I hold psychiatry, its works and its pomps, is the reason why I still haven't dared look into what became of Nadja. I've said why I was pessimistic about her fate, and about the fate of those like her. Treated in a private facility with all the care lavished on the rich, not subjected to harmful crowding but rather comforted appropriately by the presence of friends, her wishes granted as much as possible, gradually brought back to an acceptable sense of reality, which means not rushing her but allowing her to rediscover on her own the source of her disturbance: I might be sticking my neck out, but I have every reason to believe she could have gotten over this trouble. But Nadja was poor, which in our time is enough to condemn her the moment she dares to be not entirely in conformity with the imbecilic code of good sense and good behavior. And she was alone: "Sometimes it's terrible to be so alone. You're my only friends," she told my wife over the phone, the last time. In the end, her strength, and her weakness (as one can be weak), was her belief in an idea she'd always held but in which I too readily encouraged her, helped her to give it primacy over any other: the idea that freedom, acquired here on earth at the cost of a thousand difficult sacrifices, demands that we enjoy it unreservedly and without any practical considerations in the time we have it; that human emancipation—conceived in its simplest revolutionary form, which is nonetheless human emancipation *in every respect*, that is, *according to each person's means*—remains the only cause worth serving. Nadja was born to serve it, if only by demonstrating that every individual must foment a private conspiracy, which doesn't exist solely in his imagination, and which it would be wise, just from the standpoint of knowledge, to take into account; but also, and much more dangerously, by passing her head, then her arm, through the bars of logic, that most hateful of prisons, which this knowledge has pulled apart.

It was on the road to that last undertaking that perhaps I should have held her back, but first I would have had to realize the risk she was courting. Now, I never thought that she might lose or had already lost that minimal common sense which dictates that, all things considered, my friends and I *stand up* when a flag goes past, for instance, merely refraining from saluting it; or that we don't always take to task whomever we feel like; or that we might not allow ourselves the incomparable thrill of committing a lovely sacrilege; etc. It might not say much for my powers of judgment, but I confess that I didn't see anything outlandish when Nadja, for instance, handed me a letter signed "Henri Becque," in which the dramatist offered advice. If the advice was unfavorable to me, I merely answered, "Becque was a smart man, he would never have told you that." But I completely understood that, because she was drawn to the bust of Becque in Place Villiers and liked his facial expression, she should want, and manage to get, his opinion on certain matters. At very least, nothing about this is any more irrational than seeking guidance from a saint or some deity. Nor did Nadja's letters, which I read in the same way that I read all sorts of surrealist texts, present anything I found alarming. I will add just a few words in my defense. The well-known absence of boundaries between *non-madness* and madness dissuades me from assigning different values to perceptions or ideas produced by the former or the latter. There are sophisms that are infinitely more meaningful and far-reaching than the most commonly accepted truths. To dismiss them as mere sophisms is lacking in both breadth and interest. If sophisms they indeed were, then let's at least admit that they did more than anything to make me shout out to myself, to the person who from so far away is coming to meet me, the patently pathetic cry, "Who goes there?" Who goes there? Is it you, Nadja? Is it true that the *beyond*, all the beyond, is contained in this life? I can't hear you. Who's there? Is it only me? Is it myself?

I ENVY (in a manner of speaking) anyone who has time to prepare something like a book, and who, coming to the end of it, can still take an interest in the fate of the thing, or the fate it may ultimately visit upon him. If only I could believe that, along the way, he'd had at least one good opportunity to abandon it! Having got beyond that, perhaps he might do us the honor of telling us why. However tempted I might be to undertake something that requires breath, I'm too certain of being unworthy of life as I love it and as it offers itself: life that *leaves you breathless*. The sudden spaces between words in even a printed sentence; the line we draw when speaking under a certain number of propositions that cannot be summed up; the elision of events that, practically overnight, upend the particulars of a problem we thought we could solve; the indeterminable emotional coefficient that both the remotest ideas and the most concrete memories that we seek to express take on and discharge over time: given all this, I no longer have the heart to focus on anything but the interval separating these last few lines from the ones on which this book, as I leaf through it, appeared to end two pages ago.* A very brief and negligible interval for the reader,

*Similarly, in a moment of idleness on the Quai du Vieux-Port in Marseille, shortly before sundown, I once watched an oddly scrupulous painter struggle

whether or not he's reading quickly, but, I admit, one that is out of proportion and of inestimable value for me. How can I make myself understood? If I were to reread this story, with the patient and somewhat disinterested eye that I'm sure I'd have, I don't know how much of it I'd let stand, given how I currently feel about myself. I do not wish to know. I prefer to think that between the end of August, when I stopped writing it, and the end of December, when this story, finding me bent under the weight of an infinitely greater emotion, tears loose from me and becomes frightening, I've lived through—well or poorly, as one can—the greatest hopes it could have given me and then, believe me or not, through the very realization, the full realization, yes, the *implausible* realization of those hopes. This is why the voice speaking in it still deserves to be heard, in human terms, and why I do not disavow the few rare accents I've put into it. Whereas Nadja, the person of Nadja, is so far away... As are a few others. And, brought by the Marvel, or perhaps already reclaimed by it—the Marvel in which my faith has not wavered from the first page of this book to the last—a name that is no longer hers chimes in my ear.

I began by revisiting some of the places where this narrative happens to lead. My hope was to provide a photographic

---

speedily and dexterously against the fading light. The area on his canvas that corresponded to the sun gradually lowered as the sun set. In the end, nothing was left. The painter suddenly found himself lagging well behind. He removed the red from a wall, got rid of a few glints remaining on the water. His painting, which for him was finished and for me unfinished in the extreme, struck me as very sad and very beautiful.

I envy (in a manner of speaking) anyone who has time to prepare something like a book (p. 111)

image of those places, as well as of individuals or objects, that would show the exact perspective from which I had viewed them. But I realized that, with few exceptions, they resisted my attempts, and I find the illustrations in *Nadja* highly disappointing: Becque surrounded by sinister fencing, the management of the Théâtre Moderne on its guard, Pourville dead and disenchanting like no other town in France, the disappearance of practically anything having to do with *The Trail of the Octopus*. Especially frustrating, as I was particularly keen on it (even though it is not otherwise mentioned in the book), was the inability to get permission to photograph an adorable wax figure that can be seen at the Grévin Wax Museum, to the left, when you go from the room with modern political celebrities to the one featuring, behind a curtain in back, an evening at the theater: a woman fastening her garter in the shadows, which to my knowledge is the only statue with eyes, the eyes of provocation, etc.*

*I had not realized until now all the ways in which Nadja's attitude toward me pertains to the application of a more or less conscious principle of total subversion, of which I'll relate this one example: one evening, as I was driving from Versailles to Paris, a woman at my side, who was Nadja but who could in fact have been someone else, even *that* someone—her foot pressing mine on the gas pedal, her hands trying to cover my eyes in the oblivion of an endless kiss—wanted us to no longer exist, except for each other and for all eternity, as we hurtled toward a collision with the splendid trees. What a test of love! No need to add that I did not yield to this desire: we know how I felt then toward Nadja, and how I believe I have almost always felt. I am no less grateful to her for having revealed to me, in such a terribly gripping way, what a mutual acknowledgment of love would have committed us to at that moment. I feel less and less capable of resisting similar temptations *in any case*. I can do no less than give thanks, vis-à-vis this last memory, to her who made me understand how nearly necessary it was. In situations of extreme challenge, certain rare individuals, who can expect everything and fear everything from each other, will always recognize each other. In my imagination, at least, I often find myself, eyes blindfolded, at the wheel of that runaway car. Just as my friends are the ones

While boulevard Bonne-Nouvelle seemed to answer my expectations—unfortunately when I was away from Paris—during those magnificent days of pillage in support of Sacco and Vanzetti, standing out as one of the truly great strategic points that I seek in the realm of disorder (I persist in believing that such landmarks are obscurely provided to me, as to anyone who readily yields to inexplicable urges, so long as this involves an absolute sense of love or revolution and naturally entails the negation of everything else)—while boulevard Bonne-Nouvelle, then, the facades of its cinemas painted over, has since fallen silent and still, as if the Porte Saint-Denis had just closed shut, I also saw reopen and then again close the Théâtre des Deux-Masques, its name reduced to just one mask, still on rue Fontaine but now only half the distance from my apartment. Etc. It's a queer thing, as that abominable gardener said. But so goes the external world, that cock-and-bull story. That's the climate we're in; I wouldn't put a dog out in it.

I'm not one to ponder what has become of "the shape of a city," not even of the real city that is distracted and abstracted from the one I live in by dint of an element that is to my thinking what air purportedly is to life. At present, I watch without regret as it becomes other and pulls away. It slips, it burns, it sinks into the trembling wild grasses of its barricades, into the dream of its curtains, in a room where a man and a woman obliviously go on making love. I leave unfinished this mental landscape whose limits I find so disheartening, despite its astonishing extension toward Avi-

---

with whom I'm sure to find *refuge* when my head is worth its weight in gold, and who run a huge risk by taking me in—they owe me only the tragic hope that I place in them—in the same way, when it comes to love, there is no doubt that, under the right conditions, I would resume that nocturnal ride.

gnon, where the Palace of the Popes has not suffered from the winter evenings and driving rain, where an old bridge ended up collapsing under a nursery rhyme, where a marvelous and inviolable hand pointed out to me, not so long ago, a huge sky-blue road sign bearing the words: THE DAWNS; despite this extension and all the others, which help me plant a star in the very heart of the *finite*. I foresee, and no sooner is this established than I've already foreseen. Be that as it may, if one has to wait, if one has to be sure, if one has to take precautions, if one has to give the devil his due, and only his due, I categorically refuse. May the great, resounding recklessness that inspires my only decisive actions, in the only sense I can endorse, forever make unlimited use of me. I gladly renounce any opportunity to take back what I hereby give it anew. Once again, I wish to recognize only that recklessness, to depend on it alone and roam its vast piers almost at my leisure, staring at a bright spot that I know exists in my own eye and that saves me from colliding with its nocturnal freight.

Someone once told me a joke that was so somber, stupid, and deeply moving. One day, a man walks into a hotel and asks for a room. They give him number 35. Coming back downstairs a few minutes later, while handing the key back to the reception: "Pardon me," he says. "I have no memory. If you wouldn't mind, every time I come back in, I'll tell you my name, Mr. Delouit,* and you repeat my room number to me."—"Very good, sir." Shortly afterward, he comes back to the reception desk: "Mr. Delouit."—"Number 35."—"Thank you." A minute later, an utterly distraught figure, his clothes covered in mud, soaked in blood and practically without a

*I don't know how this name is spelled.

human face, staggers up to the reception: "Mr. Delouit."—"What do you mean, 'Mr. Delouit'? Don't try to pull a fast one. Mr. Delouit just went upstairs."—"My apologies, it's me. I just fell out the window. Could you please tell me my room number?"

It was this joke that I, too, succumbed to the desire to tell *you*, when I barely knew you, O you who must no longer remember, but who, having by chance read the beginning of this book, stepped so fortuitously, so violently, so effectively into my life, no doubt to remind me that I wanted it to "swing like a door" and that through that door I would never see anyone enter but you. Anyone enter and exit but you. You, who from everything I've said here will take away only a little rain on your hand as it pointed to THE DAWNS. You, who make me so regret having written that absurd and irrefutable sentence about love, the only kind of love, "that can overcome any obstacle." You, who, for anyone listening, must be not an entity but a woman, who are nothing so much as a woman, despite everything about you that has urged me and urges me still to turn you into a chimera. You, who do everything you do so admirably; whose splendid reasons, which I do not think verge on unreason, come shooting down, brilliant and lethal as lightning. You, the most vital of creatures, who seem to have been put on my path solely to make me feel the full power of what you do not feel. You, who know evil only by hearsay. You, naturally, ideally beautiful. You, whom everything relates to daybreak, which means that I might never see you again . . .

What will I do, without you, with that love of genius that

I've always felt, in whose name I've tried to recognize a few individuals? I pride myself on knowing where that genius lies, almost what it consists of, and I deemed it capable of reconciling all the other great fervors. I believe blindly in your genius. If that word shocks you, I'll reluctantly retract it—but in that case, I want to banish it entirely. Genius... what more could I possibly expect from the few possible *intercessors* who have appeared to me under this sign, and who vanished once you were here!

Without intending to, you have taken the place of the forms most familiar to me, as well as of several premonitory figures. Nadja was among the latter, and it is fitting that you have obscured her for me.

All I know is that this replacement of persons stops with you, because nothing can replace you, and for me it was with you that this succession of terrible or charming enigmas had to end once and for all.

You are not an enigma for me.

I mean to say that you have turned me away from enigmas forever.

Since you exist, as only you know how to *exist*, perhaps it was not so necessary for this book to exist. I decided it might be otherwise, in memory of the conclusion I wanted to give it before knowing you, which your irruption into my life did not rob of its meaning. That conclusion even takes on its true significance and all its power only through you.

It smiles at me as you have sometimes smiled at me, from behind great thickets of tears. "It's still love," you said; and more unfairly, you've also had occasion to say: "All or nothing."

I will never contradict that expression, with which passion definitively took up arms as it sallied forth to save the world from itself. At most, I would venture to question the nature of that "all," were it not for the fact that passion, because it is passion, cannot understand what I mean by that. How could its *varied reactions*, even as I suffer from them—and regardless of whether passion could ever deprive me of speech, cancel my right to exist—entirely strip me of the pride of knowing it, of the absolute humility I wish to feel before it, and it alone? I will not appeal its harshest and most mystifying edicts. You may as well try to stop the course of the world by virtue of some illusory power that passion confers over it. May as well deny that "each one wills and believes himself better than the world in which he is; but he who is better, only expresses his world better than others express it."*

A certain attitude toward beauty necessarily results from this, beauty that is conceived here solely in terms of passion. It is in no way static, in other words encased in its "dream of stone," lost for mankind in the shadow of Odalisques, behind those tragedies that claim to encompass only a single day; nor is it dynamic, in other words subject to that rampant gallop after which there is only another rampant gallop, in other words more scattered than a snowflake in a blizzard, in other words determined never to let itself be embraced, for fear of being confined: neither dynamic nor static, I see beauty as I have seen you. As I have seen what—at a given hour and for a given time, which I hope and believe with all my soul will be given again—granted you to me. It is like a train ceaselessly lurching from the Gare de Lyon, but that I

*Hegel.

know will never leave, has never left. It is made of jolts and shocks, most of which are not significant but which we know will necessarily bring about a huge *Shock*, which is significant. Which has all the significance I'd like to ascribe to myself. The mind constantly assumes rights that it doesn't have. Beauty, neither dynamic nor static. The human heart, beautiful as a seismograph. Royalty of silence ... The morning paper can always bring me news of myself:

"X., December 26.—The operator assigned to the telegraph station on *Sable Island* captured a fragmentary message, apparently sent on Sunday evening at such-and-such a time by ... The message said notably, "Something is not right," but did not specify the aircraft's position. Because of the very poor atmospheric conditions and resulting static, the operator was unable to make out any further statements or restore contact.

"The message was transmitted over a wavelength of 625 meters. Given the strength of the signal, the operator believed the location of the aircraft to be within a radius of 80 kilometers around *Sable Island*."

Beauty will be CONVULSIVE or not at all.

NOTES

3 "knowing whom I 'haunt'": Breton is referencing the old French adage (sometimes attributed, mistakenly, to him or to Marcel Duchamp) "Tell me whom you haunt and I will tell you who you are." "Haunt" here is used in the sense of "frequent" or "seek the company of," though the text clearly plays on the more spectral meaning as well.

5 "when the column fell": The column in Place Vendôme, built in homage to Napoleon, was toppled in 1871 during the Paris Commune—a major historical reference point for Breton and many of the Surrealists—and one of the people most instrumental in this had been Citizen Gustave Courbet, who was then president of the Federation of Artists. After the Commune was suppressed, the column was rebuilt and the statue of Napoleon set back on top.

6 "transfiguration of the features": The quote comes from notes that de Chirico did publish several years later. See "Meditations of a Painter: What the Future of Painting Might Be," in Giorgio de Chirico, *Hebdomeros* (Cambridge, Mass.: Exact Change, 1992). For the 1963 edition of *Nadja*, Breton added a footnote to this effect.

6 "any of my friends": The French novelist and critic Joris-Karl Huysmans (1848–1907) was an important precursor of Surrealism and a lifelong reference for Breton, who included excerpts from Huysmans's work in his *Anthology of Black Humor* (1940). His best-known books are *En rade* (*Stranded*), *Là-bas* (*Down There*), and, especially, *À rebours* (*Against Nature*).

8 "tics, tics, and tics": At the time *Nadja* was written, almost nothing was known about Isidore Ducasse, the self-styled Comte de Lautréamont, apart from the two works he'd left behind, *Maldoror* (1869) and *Poésies* (1870), both of seminal importance to the Surrealist movement. Breton had hand-copied *Poésies* from the only known copy, in the Bibliothèque Nationale, and published it in his magazine *Littérature* in 1919, thereby perhaps saving it from oblivion. In the past several decades, more information about Ducasse has come to light, including full-length biographies by François Caradec and Jean-Jacques Lefrère and at least one verified photograph. The phrase "tics, tics, and tics" occurs in the *Poésies* as a damning summation of poets (Hugo, Corneille, Racine...) whom Ducasse found singularly unworthy.

8 "*25 Police Rantings*": Breton is recalling the tumultuous performance of Tzara's play *The Gas Heart* on July 16, 1923 (at the so-called Evening of the Bearded Heart), which several future Surrealists in the audience tried to disrupt. In response, Tzara called the police on the troublemakers, which Breton and friends deemed the lowest form of ignominy, and which sealed the two men's breakup for the next six years. In the 1963 edition, these disputes long past, Breton deleted the sentence beginning "Mr. Tristan Tzara."

10 "hunting with eagle owls": In this method of hunting, an owl is placed in the hunting grounds of birds of prey, who flock toward it to chase it away. The hunter, hidden in a shack or behind a blind, can then pick them off. From the Manoir d'Ango, Breton wrote to his wife on August 5, 1927: "This morning, they offered to set up a table for me in a nearby field or wood, inside a small hut. The proprietor offered to lend me his rifle so that I could hunt birds of prey with an eagle owl, without having to leave the table where I'm reading or writing."

14 "chatting with Picasso": Louis Aragon later claimed that Breton was actually chatting with the writer Jean Paulhan, and that he changed it in *Nadja* because he was feuding with Paulhan at the time. Aragon might be misremembering about the chat,

but the "mutual acquaintance" mentioned a few lines later was indeed Paulhan, whose name was erased from the original edition but restored in the 1963 revision, which reads: "Not long afterward, via Jean Paulhan, I began corresponding with Paul Éluard, without either of us having the slightest notion of the other's physical appearance."

14 "walking with Soupault": *The Magnetic Fields*, written jointly by Breton and Philippe Soupault in the spring of 1919 and published in book form in 1920, was entirely composed of automatic writings produced by various means. It is widely considered the first Surrealist text proper, created five years before Breton wrote and published the *Manifesto of Surrealism*. The last page of the book is in fact formatted as a faux advertisement: "André Breton & Philippe Soupault / WOOD & COAL." In 1968, Louis Aragon reminisced: "When I knew A.B., nothing irritated him like the advertisements on the walls of Paris buildings for 'Charbons Breton,' and this at a time when, after three years of war, all the posters were in shreds—except for that miserable coal."

19 "the *sleeping fits*": During these sessions, mainly held in the Bretons' studio in the autumn of 1922, various participants appeared to fall into a hypnotic trance and uttered phrases that Breton and the others considered both oracular and remarkable instances of spontaneous poetry. The two most assiduous practitioners were the poets René Crevel, who introduced the sessions to the group, and Robert Desnos, who eventually became so dependent on them that Breton had to halt the experiment. See Breton's account in "The Mediums Enter" (1922), in *The Lost Steps* (Lincoln: University of Nebraska Press, 1996), and Simone Breton's contemporary descriptions in Simone Breton, *Lettres à Denise Lévy, 1919–1929* (Paris: Editions Joëlle Losfeld, 2005).

21 "*The Trail of the Octopus*": The serial thriller, which actually comprised fifteen episodes, was directed by Duke Worne and released in 1919; the scene Breton describes was in fact in the fifteenth, not the eighth. Breton and many of his friends retained a lifelong passion for these silent-era serials, most notably Louis

Feuillade's *Fantômas* (1913–14) and *Les Vampires* (1915), the latter starring Musidora (stage name of Jeanne Roques) as the body-stockinged femme fatale Irma Vep.

24 "I *follow* too loosely": Breton is playing on the ambiguity of the phrase "je suis," which can mean both "I follow" and, looping back to the beginning of the book, "I am."

24 "Passage de l'Opéra": This was one of many covered gallerias honeycombing the Right Bank of Paris, mostly in the second and ninth arrondissements, in the area around the Paris Opéra and the city's northern boulevards. Many had been demolished by 1926, including the one in question, though some notable ones still remain as of this writing. When Tristan Tzara brought the Dada movement to Paris in 1920, enlisting a number of the future Surrealists, the group's daily meeting place was Café Certâ, also in the Passage de l'Opéra. Aragon's *Paris Peasant* (1926) contains a lengthy and detailed homage to the galleria and its delightfully tawdry commerce.

27 "salon at the bottom of a lake": The phrase is from Rimbaud's *A Season in Hell.*

32 "some demon, no doubt": Though Breton did not know it at the time, a third authorial presence in *The Deranged* (*Les Détraquées*), along with the "surgeon named Thierry" [*sic*] and the actor Pierre Palau, was the neurologist Joseph Babinski, under whom Breton had served as a medical orderly during the First World War. For the 1963 edition, he added this footnote: "The true identity of these authors was not revealed until thirty years later. It was only in 1956 that the periodical *Le Surréalisme, même* was able to publish the complete text of *The Deranged* with an afterword by P.-L. Palau that shed light on its genesis: 'The initial idea was inspired by some dubious incidents that had occurred in a girls' school in the Paris suburbs. But given the theater for which I intended it—the Deux-Masques—which mainly staged Grand Guignol, I had to play up the melodramatic side, while respecting absolute scientific accuracy: the scabrous nature of what I was writing about demanded it. It was about a case of *folie circulaire*

with free intervals [today called bipolar disorder], but to do it right required knowledge that I didn't possess. It was then that a friend of mine, Dr. Paul Thiéry, a surgeon at the hospital, put me in touch with the eminent Joseph Babinski, who was glad to enlighten me; this allowed me to treat the so-called scientific portion of the play free of errors.' Great was my surprise to learn that Dr. Babinski had taken part in the development of *The Deranged*. I've kept a warm memory of the illustrious neurologist, having assisted him, as a 'temporary intern,' for an extended period at La Pitié Hospital. I have always felt honored by the friendliness he showed me—even though he was misguided enough to predict for me a great future in medicine!—and, in return, I believe I put his teachings to good use; the end of the first *Manifesto of Surrealism* pays homage to them."

33 "to my great shame": Breton added this footnote to the 1963 edition: "What did I mean by that? Only that I should have gone up to her, done everything in my power to discover the *woman* she truly was. To do that, I would have had to overcome a certain prejudice against actresses, fostered by the memory of Vigny and Nerval. I accuse myself of having failed 'passionate attraction.'" The latter expression is from Charles Fourier, whose work Breton discovered in the 1940s during his wartime exile in New York.

35 "very great, very keen emotion": For the 1963 edition, Breton revised this passage to read: "The power of enchantment that Rimbaud exerted over me around 1915, and which, since then, has become epitomized in rare poems such as 'Devotion,' is no doubt what caused me at the time, one day as I was walking alone under the driving rain, to meet a girl who came up to me and, without preamble, as we were walking side by side, offered to recite..." And he added this footnote, after "enchantment": "The word 'enchantment' must be taken strictly literally. For me, the outside world was constantly merging with his world, which, even more so, placed a *grid* over it: on my daily route at the outskirts of a city that was Nantes, dazzling correspondences were established with his city somewhere else. I 'recognized' corners of villas, their

stretches of lawn, as if through his eyes; creatures that had seemed alive a second earlier suddenly slipped into his wake, etc."

39 "Her name is Fanny Beznos": Note added to the 1963 edition: "Reviewing these notations, some disappoint me more than others: what did I actually expect from her? It's only that Surrealism was still seeking itself, was still a long way from defining itself as a conception of the world. Unable to predict how much time it had left, it groped its way forward and was perhaps too satisfied with its early radiance. Without a beam of shadow, no beam of light." Born into a Russian Jewish family in 1907, Beznos was already a committed political activist by the time of her encounter with Breton. Her revolutionary militancy caused her to be deported to Belgium in 1929 and, when the war broke out, to be placed on a police blacklist. Arrested in Paris in 1941, she was tortured and sent to Auschwitz, where she was murdered in October 1942.

39 "the Surrealist Central": The Bureau of Surrealist Research, or Surrealist Central, was a walk-in storefront that the fledgling group opened on October 11, 1924, at 15 rue de Grenelle, as part of the movement's launch campaign (Breton's *Manifesto* was published four days later). Although it eventually succumbed to a lack of commitment and discipline on the part of those who were charged with maintaining it, its fitful six-month existence led to several significant encounters—including with the poet Lise Meyer (Lise Deharme), the "lady of the glove," for whom Breton conceived an unrequited passion that lasted through the writing of *Nadja*. Though Deharme never gave in to Breton's courtship, the two remained lifelong friends.

39 "read as POLICE": Footnote added to the 1963 edition: "'At a certain oblique angle': it would take several years, on the occasion of certain 'trials,' for the uniquely tragic collusion manifested by the chance juxtaposition of these two words to become fully evident. The beast that can be seen head-on in the following lines is, indeed, the one that common convention describes as 'bloodthirsty.'—The fact that it was precisely that person's index finger pointing to the sign in Pourville is not, in retrospect, with-

out a rather cruel irony." The "trials" Breton is referring to are the so-called Moscow Show Trials, instigated by Stalin between 1936 and 1938, which Breton was among the first leftist intellectuals in France to denounce. Shortly before this, in 1932, Aragon, he of the pointing finger, had split bitterly from the Surrealist movement to join the Stalinists and by the time of the 1963 edition had become a prominent member of the French Communist Party, to Breton's undying rancor.

42 "*to be earned by work*": This rebuttal of the "moral value" of work directly reflects Breton's troubled relations at the time with the Communist Party, which he had briefly joined in early 1927, and with which he maintained turbulent relations until 1935, when he broke with the Stalinists once and for all. No doubt at the forefront of Breton's mind when composing this passage was a cell meeting from several months earlier, during which he was tarred as an "idler" and "carouser" for his refusal to honor the sanctity of labor.

43 "Trotsky's latest volume": *L'Humanité* was, and remains, the house organ of the French Communist Party. The fact that Trotsky's books were available at its bookstore is a reminder that in the fall of 1926, Trotsky was still considered a full-fledged member of the Soviet leadership. One year later, he would be expelled from the Party, and in 1940 assassinated under orders from Stalin. Breton and his second wife, the painter Jacqueline Lamba, visited Trotsky, in exile in Mexico, in 1938.

46 "only the beginning": In the manuscript, Nadja's explanation (which likely represents her actual words) reads: "because in Russian it more or less means hope, and because it only means it more or less." When revising the manuscript, Breton crossed out this line and inserted the final wording.

51 "not Lena, Nadja": Is it worth pointing out that Lena is a variant of Léona, Nadja's real first name?

52 "Dutch candies": According to Hester Albach, a slang term for drugs, specifically opium squares that look like the coffee-flavored sweets called *hopjes*.

54 "pages have been cut open": At the time, French books were sold with the pages uncut, which among other things allowed one to see how far (or whether) the recipient of a copy had read in it.

55 "Soluble Fish": This was Breton's second book-length manuscript of automatic prose, written in the spring of 1924. Disappointed by the lack of attention that had greeted *The Magnetic Fields* in 1920, he planned to endow his new book with a theoretical preface that would clue the reader in to the work's significance. Over the following months, the preface ballooned into the *Manifesto of Surrealism*, which was published in October 1924, with "Soluble Fish" as an appendix.

60 "'that carried a threat'": A drawing by Nadja from around this time, a portrait of Breton with a serpent encircling his face, is captioned "The kiss that kills."

62 "Urget aquas vis sursum eadem...": The caption, which translates as "The same force that propels the water upward also makes it fall back again," illustrates the end of Berkeley's Third Dialogue: "You see, *Hylas*, the water of yonder fountain, how it is forced upwards, in a round column, to a certain height; at which it breaks, and falls back into the basin from whence it rose: its ascent as well as descent proceeding from the same uniform law or principle of *gravitation*. Just so, the same principles which, at first view, lead to Scepticism, pursued to a certain point, bring men back to Common Sense."

67 "*The Profanation of the Host*": This predella painting (1465–69) by Paolo Uccello is more commonly known as *The Miracle of the Desecrated Host*, though we can see why the staunchly anticlerical Breton would have preferred the alternate title. Salvador Dalí painted his own *Profanation of the Host* around 1930, at the height of his involvement with Surrealism, quite likely in response to Breton's admiration of Uccello.

69 "*La Révolution surréaliste*": The first of many magazines produced by the Paris Surrealist group in its nearly fifty years of existence, *La Révolution surréaliste* lasted for twelve issues, between

December 1924 and December 1929, at which point it was replaced by *Le Surréalisme au service de la révolution*—the movement having switched from *being* the Revolution to *serving* it, at least in slogan.

79 "Madame de Chevreuse": For the 1963 edition, Breton rewrote this passage to read: "We are forced to wait for the next train, which will drop us off in Saint-Germain at around one o'clock. Walking past the château, Nadja saw herself as Madame de Chevreuse..."—eliding both their night in the hotel and, earlier, the specificity of their first-class train compartment, which they had taken in a vain bid for privacy. Similarly, several pages later, Breton replaced the phrase "the last time I visited her" with the more ambiguous "the last time we met." In a preface written for the new edition, Breton justified these revisions as an attempt to "try to obtain a little more aptness in terminology, and fluidity in other respects... After thirty-five years... the slight retouchings that I have decided to make to [the text] evidence only a certain concern with saying it better." Similarly, the late-generation Surrealist Claude Courtot recalled Breton saying that he had "noticed on rereading the book that there were some little stylistic flaws, some lapses of taste." Whether these changes are indeed merely stylistic is for the reader to judge.

80 "a single couple": Jean-Antoine Watteau's painting *L'Embarquement pour Cythère* (Louvre, 1717), also known as *Voyage to Cythera*, depicts amorous couples (or, as Breton suggests, repetitions of the same couple in different poses) about to depart from the island of Cythera, birthplace of Venus.

84 "jotted down in my presence": Many of these phrases appear, in slightly altered form, in letters that Nadja sent to Breton in the autumn and winter of 1926–27 (see introduction).

95 "the best of all": This drawing was not in fact lost but had been among the papers kept for generations by Nadja's family. It resurfaced at a public auction in 2019 and was published in 2020 in the catalog *L'Invention du surréalisme.*

104 "like that Professor Claude": For readers of *Nadja,* Dr. Henri Claude has long stood as the prototype of scientific narrow-mindedness. As a medical intern, Breton had attended Claude's lectures in the Sainte-Anne amphitheater, coming away from them with a profound distaste for the man's air of "obtuse superiority." But while his description of the analyst's blunt interrogation tactics is likely accurate, he also implies that Claude similarly browbeat Nadja at Sainte-Anne (in fact, he never treated her), and he fails to mention that Claude pioneered the introduction in France of Freudian psychoanalysis, which Breton admired throughout his life.

106 "an obvious and... in public": In the 1963 edition, this passage reads: "an abnormal action that can be objectively certified and is of criminal nature the moment it is committed in public..." Breton reproduced a report from the *Annales Médico-Psychologiques* that specifically condemned this passage of *Nadja* as the preamble to his *Second Manifesto of Surrealism* (1930).

108 "already lost... flag goes past": In the 1963 edition, this passage reads: "had already lost the *favor* of that instinct for self-preservation—to which I referred earlier—which dictates that, all things considered, my friends and I *stand up*—limiting ourselves to turning aside—when a flag goes past."

108 "offered advice": The dramatist Henri Becque had died in 1899, three years almost to the day before Nadja was born.

112 "under the weight... lived through": In the 1963 edition, this passage reads: "under the weight of an emotion concerning, this time, the heart much more than the mind, tears loose from me and leaves me trembling, I've lived through..."

114 "to photograph... eyes of provocation": In the 1963 edition (which does include a photo of the wax figure's thigh), this passage reads: "to photograph the adorable lure that is, at the Grévin Wax Museum, the woman pretending to retreat into the shadows to fasten her garter, and who, in her immutable pose, is the only statue I know of to have *eyes*: the eyes of provocation itself."

115 "the shape of a city": The line is from Baudelaire's poem "The Swan": "the shape of a city / Is quick to change; less so the human heart."

117 "that love of genius": A possible allusion to Rimbaud's poem "Genius" from *Illuminations*, understood as "a personification or embodiment especially of a quality or condition," akin to the genius loci. More directly, Breton, in a letter to Emmanuel Berl from late September 1928, calls Suzanne Muzard ("you"; see introduction) a "genius of love." See also his earlier characterization of Nadja as "a free genius."

118 "most familiar to me": Among the "most familiar" forms Suzanne Muzard has replaced, we can count Breton's wife at the time, Simone Kahn Breton, as well as Lise Meyer (see above, note to page 39), who lost her privileged spot in Breton's affections after nearly three years of vain courtship. It didn't help that, shortly before Breton's meeting with Muzard, Lise had married her lover Paul Deharme, finally killing off Breton's infatuation.

119 "others express it": The phrase is taken from Benedetto Croce's *What Is Living and What Is Dead of the Philosophy of Hegel.*

119 "dream of stone": The phrase is from Baudelaire's poem "Beauty," which begins: "I'm beautiful, O mortals! like a dream of stone."

120 "Beauty will be CONVULSIVE": The formula dates possibly as far back as the French Revolution, and certainly to Adolphe Thiers's well-known declaration from 1872, "The Republic will be conservative or not at all." Breton had already previewed a version of his concluding statement in a letter to his future wife Simone Kahn in 1920: "I count myself among the disciples of the man who said, 'Criticism will be love, or not at all.'" In 1934, he would use it as the title of an essay, which would later become the first chapter of his 1937 book *Mad Love*, the third volume of a trilogy that also includes *Nadja* and *The Communicating Vessels* (1932).

OTHER NEW YORK REVIEW CLASSICS

For a complete list of titles, visit www.nyrb.com.

OĞUZ ATAY Waiting for the Fear
DIANA ATHILL Don't Look at Me Like That
HONORÉ DE BALZAC The Lily in the Valley
POLINA BARSKOVA Living Pictures
ROSALIND BELBEN The Limit
HENRI BOSCO The Child and the River
DINO BUZZATI The Betwitched Bourgeois: Fifty Stories
CRISTINA CAMPO The Unforgivable and Other Writings
CAMILO JOSÉ CELA The Hive
FRANÇOIS-RENÉ DE CHATEAUBRIAND Memoirs from Beyond the Grave, 1800–1815
AMIT CHAUDHURI A Strange and Sublime Address
LUCILLE CLIFTON Generations: A Memoir
ANTONIO DI BENEDETTO The Suicides
JEAN ECHENOZ Command Performance
FERIT EDGÜ The Wounded Age *and* Eastern Tales
GUSTAVE FLAUBERT The Letters of Gustave Flaubert
MAVIS GALLANT The Uncollected Stories of Mavis Gallant
NATALIA GINZBURG Family *and* Borghesia
JEAN GIONO The Open Road
VASILY GROSSMAN The People Immortal
ELIZABETH HARDWICK The Uncollected Essays of Elizabeth Hardwick
HENRY JAMES On Writers and Writing
TOVE JANSSON Sun City
PAUL LAFARGUE The Right to Be Lazy
JEAN-PATRICK MANCHETTE Skeletons in the Closet
JOHN McGAHERN The Pornographer
EUGENIO MONTALE Butterfly of Dinard
AUGUSTO MONTERROSO The Rest is Silence
ELSA MORANTE Lies and Sorcery
MAXIM OSIPOV Kilometer 101
PIER PAOLO PASOLINI Theorem
DOUGLAS J. PENICK The Oceans of Cruelty: Twenty-Five Tales of a Corpse-Spirit, a Retelling
ANDREY PLATONOV Chevengur
RAYMOND QUENEAU The Skin of Dreams
RUMI Water; translated by Haleh Liza Gafori
JONATHAN SCHELL The Village of Ben Suc
ANNA SEGHERS The Dead Girls' Class Trip
ANTON SHAMMAS Arabesques
WILLIAM GARDNER SMITH The Stone Face
VLADIMIR SOROKIN Blue Lard
ITALO SVEVO A Very Old Man
MAGDA SZABÓ The Fawn
ELIZABETH TAYLOR Mrs Palfrey at the Claremont
SUSAN TAUBES Lament for Julia
TEFFI Other Worlds: Peasants, Pilgrims, Spirits, Saints
YŪKO TSUSHIMA Woman Running in the Mountains
LISA TUTTLE My Death
IVAN TURGENEV Fathers and Children
PAUL VALÉRY Monsieur Teste
MARKUS WERNER The Frog in the Throat
XI XI Mourning a Breast